Bitch Berserker: LitRPG Dark Fantasy

Bitch Berserker, Volume 1

Adam Drake

Published by Adam Drake, 2018.

BITCH BERSERKER: LITRPG DARK FANTASY

First edition. August 21, 2018.

ISBN: 979-8201453312

Written by Adam Drake.

Bitch Berserker
by
Adam Drake
Copyright © 2018 Adam Drake

Bitch Berserker

Trapped in a savage new reality!

I'm a kind and gentle person.

Or should I say, I was...

As an interstellar surveyor, my job is to find and explore new star systems at the very fringes of humankind's reach. There are no conflicts, or even stress – it's simply a career which allows me to quietly drift through the cosmos, enjoying its endless beauty.

Then I found myself trapped on a world like no other. Dark, bloody and brutal, I had to adapt quickly to this new reality, or me and my crew would never get a chance to escape. My life quickly morphed from one of peace, to one of pure savagery.

And as I carved a blood-soaked path across this realm of carnage, there was one horrifying fact about myself I needed to confront:

Learning to kill was easy, but learning not to love it so much... now that's hard.

NOTE: A LitRPG dark fantasy. Contains violence and gore.

CHAPTER ONE

"Trans-light jump completed. Internal systems now at normal. Time to wake up, Captain."

The voice drew me out of my sleep and I opened my eyes. Bright light made me quickly shut them, again. "Do you need to have the lights on so high? You know it hurts." From where I lay, I shielded my face with an arm, grumpy as a teenager woken by an alarm.

"My apologies," the voice said, sounding genuinely remorseful. "But this helps with your retinal stimulation. It's standard procedure. Especially after such a long jump. Besides, you've done this hundreds of times before."

I slowly pried my eyes open. The bright lights nearly blinded me. "Just because it's procedure doesn't mean I have to like it."

With an effort, I sat up in the sleeping pod and carefully squinted at my surroundings.

The hibernation chamber was compact with the pod at its center. I was the only one present. A wide circular door sat closed to one side. Something about the door being closed bothered me, but my sleep addled brain refused to share why.

After a few seconds of me yawning and stretching, the voice said, "What is my name?" It emanated from nowhere, yet everywhere.

"Your name?" I said, befuddled. "Why would you ask me that of all things?" I looked over to the meal nook and was delighted to see a hot bulb of coffee appear within it.

"Part of the procedure, Captain. Please answer, if you can."

If I can? What did he mean by that? Shrugging on a light robe, I said, "Otto. Your name is Otto. Now, can I have my coffee?" I padded over to the nook and eagerly took the bulb, its bottom heavily weighted to prevent tipping.

"Very good," Otto said. "Now, what is your name?"

"Zyra Hendricks," I said. This part of the questioning I knew by heart. Before Otto could ask, I quickly added, "Born on Beta-Prime Station over Pluto. Birth date January 18th, 2214. See? I remember." I breathed in the smell of the coffee before taking a sip and smiled. Lots of cream and sugar. Just the way I liked it.

"Good," Otto said. "What is your designation?"

"Captain," I said after another savory sip. "You already called me by that when you woke me, so no surprise there." I knew Otto hadn't made a mistake with this. As the ship's artificial intelligence, he rarely made mistakes. It was all part of his little wake up test.

"Of course," Otto said. "What was are last system of departure?"

As I drank the delicious coffee my eyes went to the door again. "Why's the door closed?" Then I noticed the blue light above it. "Is it sealed?"

"I will get to that in a moment," Otto said.

Before he could say more I cut him off. "No, please get to it now, Otto." I didn't think I snapped at him. I hadn't drunk enough coffee for that.

After a noticeable pause, the AI said, "The Trans-light effects on the outer hull is taking more time to dissipate. The seal is simply a precaution. No need to be alarmed. It's part of the-."

"Standard procedures," I finished for him and downed the last of the coffee. I placed the cup into the meal nook and ordered a second. "Durana 138."

"Beg pardon?" Otto said.

I arched a brow at the ceiling. "Don't get cute with me. That was our system of departure. Durana 138. Proxima Station... 4?"

"Very good. And where are you now?"

"Somewhere in the deepest parts of space, I'd assume," I said, snatching up the new coffee and taking a deep sip.

"Very funny."

"Well, I'm not wrong, am I?" I said, as I ordered a breakfast. My stomach was rumbling.

"No, you are correct. But where are you sitting now?"

I frowned when a breakfast tray didn't appear immediately. When I tried to order it again the nook emitted a chastising buzz. "Hey, what's the deal? Don't tell me these are down."

"The meal nook is functioning properly," Otto said, his voice neutral. "But until the full effects of the Trans-light jump are gone, it's best to stick with liquid intakes, only."

"But I'm hungry now," I moaned, resting my head against the meal nook.

Otto ignored my plight. "Please answer the question, Captain."

I pondered how long I could tease him, but knew how futile that would be. With a sigh, I said, "I'm in a hibernation chamber in the belly of a spaceship."

"Which ship?"

"Corena IV. Interstellar Class B," I said, a little annoyed. Maybe the coffee was getting to me.

"Perfect. Thank you, Captain."

"How are the rest of the crew?" I said, walking over to a closet with my uniform hanging inside. I fingered the fabric and, not for the first time, marveled at its texture.

"All are well. First shift is recovering from the Trans-light sleep while Second shift are still in hibernation."

Did they get breakfast? I wanted to ask, as I pulled on the uniform. I never liked its colors of blue on white. But those were corporation colors, so one couldn't argue. "And the engines?"

"Cooling down within normal parameters. No spikes. Radial plates expelling heat at optimal limit."

"Good. Wouldn't want us to implode as soon as we arrived," I said, smoothing on my uniform. These things never wrinkled and I liked the feel of the fabric on my skin.

"About that."

I sighed, and arched a brow at the ceiling. "We were transiting to some numbered system, right? Don't expect me to remember it. My memory is quite patchy when I haven't eaten breakfast."

"YH 1265 is the system's designation."

I regarded the blue light over the door. "84 days of jump time, right?"

"Yes. 84 days, 16 hours and 32 minutes."

I was expecting a little more, and when the AI offered nothing, I grew concerned. "Otto. What aren't you telling me?"

"We've been in system for 6 days and 4 hours."

Whoa. "Really? Why? The aftereffects?"

"Correct. After such a long jump it wasn't safe to wake you and the crew until now."

"Wow," I said. "That's some kind of record, isn't it?" Normally, I could check for myself on a screen, but the chambers were purposely devoid of any. All a part of the corporation's protocols to soften the shock of the crew emerging from hibernation. Humankind was never meant to sleep for such long periods of time. I tried not to dwell on how much time I'd spent tucked away in a sleeping pod over the years.

"It is extreme, yes," Otto said. "But not overly dangerous. The corporation wouldn't have assigned us to this system, otherwise."

Spoken like a true corporation-owned, and corporation-progammed, AI. I rapped my knuckles on the door. "So, how long are you going to make me stay in here? We have a new system to survey." A tingle of excitement blossomed in my stomach. A new survey was the best part of the job.

The door irised open in answer.

"The ship's interior is stable," Otto said. "Please proceed. And I apologize for the delay."

"No need to," I said, stepping into the hallway beyond and noted the three doors of the other chambers were closed. Second shift still sleeping. One level below, the others of first shift would be waking.

I snatched a view tablet from the wall and checked on the others.

Active Crew:

Zyra H. - Captain / Lead Surveyor - 1st Shift – Deck 2

Caddie Y. - Astronavigator - 1st Shift – Bridge

Pullman K. - Chief Engineer – 1st Shift – Engineering

Hibernating Crew:

Abdul M. - 2nd Captain / Surveyor - 2nd Shift – Deck 2

Morris R. - Astronavigator - 2nd Shift – Deck 2

Ronald Q. - Engineer - 2nd Shift – Deck 2

"Oh, hey," I said, annoyed. "What are Caddie and Pullman doing up before me?"

"They woke up the same time as you, Captain. Only they got to their stations sooner."

"Oh, yeah? Why's that?" I said, crossing over to the yellow ladder at the end of the hall. Not being the first on the bridge irritated me to no end.

"They didn't pause for coffee."

"Ha ha, very funny," I said, and climbed. Using the elevator would have been quicker, but I found it too cramped for my liking, even if the trip was only several seconds. Besides, using the ladder was technically exercise, or so I kept telling myself.

Reaching the top, I emerged onto the bridge.

Only some of the lights were on, giving the small chamber a soothing atmosphere. A tinkling noise rippled through the air, melodic and slow as the ship's systems thought and processed.

Two of the three station chairs were empty, with Caddie already sitting in hers. She turned as I popped out of the floor.

"Captain! Good to see you awake and well. How was your sleep?" she said. As she spoke her eyes continually flew over her station panel, tapping at buttons and tickling indicators.

"Apparently long," I said, sitting at the middle station. I noticed Caddie's strawberry blonde hair was fixed in a bun. Not wanting to break the corporate dress code, I wrangled my dark ponytail into one, too. "Gimme a sitrep."

Caddie's fingers flew. "Engines are cooling fine, so no risk of boiling alive. All systems are online or about to be."

I glanced at my station's display. The communications buoy had been deployed only hours after our arrival and sat roughly two thousand kilometers starboard side. It would log all our activity and research over the coming days. Once we finished and jumped to the next designated system, the buoy would wait for the Second Team's arrival in a few months.

It would be up to Second Team to decide whether the system was worth exploiting or not. Our job was to gather and collate all the information for them. The grunt work.

"Okay, let's see what we can see," I said, and activated the main screen.

The entire wall on one side of the chamber blinked on, revealing a vast star field. Data streams crawled within little side panels. None flashed red, which was a good sign.

With a poke at my display, the field shifted and a small red star moved into its center. YH 1265.

"Anything exciting about this one?" I asked. Over the years, you learned that all red dwarfs looked pretty much the same. I was hoping for something a little different this time.

"Nope," Caddie said. "Basic C designation. Solar activity stable. Gravity well as expected."

I frowned. 84 days of sleep for a run of the mill star? Couldn't say that I was surprised. "Okay, the IS scan spotted only one planet. We got satellites there, yet?"

Otto was the one who answered. "Yes, Captain. Six were sent three days ago and are arriving as we speak."

I frowned. "You timed First Shift for their arrival?"

"No, Captain. As I indicated, it wasn't safe to wake you before now."

I said nothing. Part of me resented being treated like a part within a machine. Otto might of thought having the crew awake before there was actual work to be done as wasteful. Not that his programming would allow him to admit as much.

Caddie brought me out of my dour thoughts. "Satellite data incoming."

The wall screen blinked, replacing the dull red dwarf with a large white ball. A planet.

I gasped in surprise and heard Caddie do the same.

The planet was unlike any I'd seen before. Absolutely white and devoid of any recognizable atmosphere. But its surface was most curious of all. Perfectly smooth without a hint of blemish. No craters, no tectonic lines, no mountain ranges. Nothing.

Caddie and I stared at the screen for several moments, mesmerized.

"Whoa," Caddie said, wide-eyed.

I agreed. This planet was wholly unique, both in my own surveys and my research training at the academy.

"Satellites are settling into their respective orbits now," Otto said.

"Any activity from the surface?" I asked. Although we couldn't see anything didn't mean something wasn't there.

"None," he said.

I blinked out of my reverie. "Otto, scan the database, please. Has the corporation every seen a planet like this?"

"No, Captain. Nothing like this has been encountered before. Not in the corporation's database, nor the shared collective archive."

I stared at the white billiard ball on the screen. How was it possible something like it could even exist? There had to be some kind of surface markings. It would be impossible for it not to. "Anything else in system?" I said, turning to Caddie.

She tore her gaze from the screen to her station display. "Negative. Nothing else in orbit that we can see."

"Nothing? What about asteroids?"

Caddie shook her head. "Nothing big enough to be seen transiting the star field. It'll take a couple of days to do a more thorough scan, but for now, this planet is the only thing here."

I looked back at the strange planet. A barren system containing a bizarre planet. Was this why the corporation sent us here?

A memory tugged at me and I pulled up the predesignated flight path schedule assigned to the Corena. Scanning it quickly showed something off. Three jumps prior, a corporation trans-light drone arrived in the system we were shore-leaved at. It contained an updated path of systems, drastically altering the one assigned before. I remember noticing the change but thought nothing of it. It wasn't unusual to have a travel change made. In fact, it was common place as competing corporations sought to outmaneuver one another in order to be the first to survey a system.

Yet now I couldn't help but look at the change as anything more than suspicious. Did the corporation spot this strange system at the last minute and scramble to send us here? Looking at the available ship log data told me we were the closest survey ship that could've reached this system, but only after a long jump.

"Whoa, it's tiny," Caddie said, snapping me out of my thoughts.

I glanced at the data. "Two thousand kilometers in diameter. That would barely constitute a moon." Looking at the other data points revealed the small planet was tidally locked with the red dwarf, and had an orbit of six hundred and twenty two Earth years.

Caddie glanced over at me with an expression of bewilderment. "What now, Captain?"

What now, indeed? Regardless of how bizarre the system was, we were there for a reason. "Well, even though we found a one-in-a-million planet doesn't mean anything has changed." I leaned forward in my seat and grinned. "Let's get down to business."

Caddie laughed and shrugged. "Suits me just fine. I'll pull up the data points on the Interstellar Scans from the previous systems and-."

"Captain!" Otto said, interrupting. "The planet!"

We looked at the giant screen.

Something was happening. The little planet appeared to be changing. No, not changing. Growing.

Confused for a moment, I said, "Is system radiation messing with the cameras?"

"Negative," Otto said.

I looked again at the planet's information, and knew it wasn't the cameras playing tricks. The planet was expanding. It was at four thousand kilometers in diameter, and increasing with every second.

Boggled, I watched as the planet continued to grow.

"What in the hell is going on?" I said, awed.

"Unknown," Otto said. "But there never has been any planet or celestial object ever recorded displaying such activity."

A growing planet? Planets didn't grow.

Alarmed, I pinged Pullman who answered immediately. His grizzled expression appearing on a side screen.

"Is it meal time, yet?" The engineer said. "Cause I didn't get any breakfast."

"How long before the trans-light drive is ready to jump?"

Caddie's mouth dropped open at the question, but I ignored her.

Pullman's calm expression morphed into concern. "Uh, five and a half days. Standard wait time. Why?"

I glanced at the planet's data, again. Seven thousand kilometers in diameter and still expanding. "What's the quickest we can get that time down to?" Like, now would be a good time.

Otto answered for the engineer. "Captain, the standard wait time is a minimum designate not only for the engines to cool, but for the safety of the crew. Humans need time to adjust before making another jump."

I knew all this. Hell, it was covered in basic training and hammered into our brains. You didn't risk your crew in order to save time. The effects on people made saving time impossible. Five and a half days was the golden number.

But I didn't think we'd have five and a half minutes, let alone days. To Pullman, I said, "We need to move upwell as fast as possible until the drives are ready. Can you switch some more energy over to the pulse engine?"

"Well, ya, I can, but why-."

"Just do it!" I said, and cut the comms.

Caddie stood, alarmed. "Captain, what's going on? Do you think it's going to explode?"

"I don't know, but we can't risk it. We need to move away, and quickly." Even at this far a distance from the planet, if the thing did go boom, it would scatter trillions of tons of debris upwell. I had no intention of getting hit by any of it.

"Caddie, spin us around one hundred and eighty degrees, then slap on the pulse engine."

The other woman blinked, but didn't move, as if frozen in fear.

"Caddie, now please." I made an effort to ratchet down the anxiety in my voice.

"Yes," she said, after a moment. "Yes, Captain." She sat in her seat and frantically tapped at her display.

Otto suddenly said, "We've just lost satellites one, two, three and four. They were the low orbiters."

The planet expanded so quickly the satellites couldn't compensate and had smashed into its bleak surface. This was all too bizarre to even fathom.

"Pulse engine on," Caddie said, her voice relatively calm, although her expression showed otherwise. "We should be at maximum speed in twenty minutes."

I frowned, watching the image of the planet. Was it about to blow up? Or was there something else going on? Another worrying thought worked through the frenzied activity in my brain.

The planet had started to expand right after the satellites at settle into their orbits. Did that mean it was reacting to their presence? How was that possible?

Unless...

A chill ran up my spine, and for the first time ever in my career as an interstellar surveyor, I wanted to be back at the depressing station around Pluto and far from this place.

"I think there's more going on here," I said, staring at the planet, fear cloying at my chest.

"More than an exploding planet?" Caddie said.

Suddenly, the ship's deck shifted beneath me and I flew across the bridge. I smashed into the far wall, barely managing to get my arms up. Falling to the floor, I heard the high-pitched braying of the alarms.

Dazed, I managed to sit up. "Sitrep!" I could see Caddie crumpled in a ball at the corner of the bridge.

Otto said, "It appears the pulse engine has been taken offline. Our forward momentum has ceased which is impossible without reverse thrust."

As I tried to understand what that meant, he said, "Captain, the ship is reversing direction."

"How..." I started to ask, but knew the answer. The planet.

With double vision, I looked at the display. The planet had stopped expanding, and was now over ten times its initial size. So it wasn't going to explode. It was doing something else.

Preparing.

"It's pulling us to it," I said.

After a brief moment, Otto said, "You are correct Captain. Fascinating. The power to capture an object from such a distance is absolutely staggering."

"Oh, I'm staggered," I said, managing to flop back into my chair. "Can we do anything with the maneuvering jets?" I had a faint hope we could at least spin out of its reach.

"Negative," Otto said. "All engines and drives are offline. Most systems are down. I'm trying to get them back up again."

"At this speed it will take almost a full day to drag us in, if that's its intent," I said.

"Agreed. I don't think the hull's integrity will hold for more than-."

Suddenly, the proximity alarms squealed to life, deafening me. The ship shook more violently than before and I found myself on the deck, again.

A whiteness filled the display wall.

The planet. It was on top of us.

"Impossible..." I heard Otto say, but the alarms and sounds of the ship's hull cracking drowned him out.

The whiteness flared in intensity, engulfing everything. In seconds, the bridge vanished. I tried to close my eyes but the whiteness was there too.

"The planet has us..." Otto's voice was barely audible.

"That's no planet," I rasped.

Then two words appeared, their black letters contrasting against the all encompassing white.

Joining Server.

CHAPTER TWO

One of the first things they taught you at the academy was that space was not empty. This tenement was always driven home to students regardless of which class we took. No matter of how monumentally vast and infinite the universe was, there was always something to find. As a surveyor, it was our job to find those 'somethings', wherever they were, and record and classify them.

For decades I believed in this unwritten law. Whichever system I was sent to, whatever far flung location I arrived at, it was never truly empty.

But I found emptiness now.

The whiteness was everything; space, the universe, my soul. It washed out all thoughts and emotions. And it was all I could do but stare into it.

Long after those two words had faded away, I was left floating in nothingness. When I tried to speak, I couldn't make words, I couldn't even make sounds. It was as if my body ceased to exist. Faded away like those words, becoming one with the great white emptiness.

The sounds of the ship cracking apart had long gone; replaced by an eerie silence, one which was somehow more deafening than the death rattle of the Corena.

Otto? I wanted to say, but could only think the name. Over and over, I mentally called out to the ship's AI, hoping for some kind of response. But none came. Occasionally, I would think the names of the crew, but the results were the same. Were they okay? Could they be in this place like me? Was this even a place at all?

My fear for my crew and ship slowly turned into a dull ache, one which couldn't be allayed. Helpless, I waited. There was nothing else I could do.

Then, without warning, the empty universe started to change. The whiteness slowly grew darker, shapes and images began to appear all around.

Confusion mixed with relief. I wasn't dead. The ship hadn't been destroyed. But what was I seeing?

Soon, blurry images began to take shape, revealing detail. But what I saw only confused me more. It was a rocky plain stretching off into the distance. Dark, angry clouds scudded overhead. Two bright orange lights became torches, stuck into the ground.

This wasn't the bridge, or any place I'd seen before. What was happening?

Otto? I tried to shout, but still couldn't verbalize. In fact, my vision was locked in place, forced to stare at the torches flickering in a wind I couldn't feel.

Panic gripped me. I couldn't understand what was going on and my lack of ability to do anything made me want to scream with frustration.

Suddenly, words appeared near the top of my vision, above the torches.

Choose your character:

Huh?

With a shock, a person appeared before me like an image on a screen.

I wanted to gasp, but couldn't.

It was me. Or at least, it was a facsimile of me. The image stood between the torches, her eyes scanning around as if looking for danger. She wore clothing made of what appeared to be thick hides. Her hair was pulled back in a tight braided ponytail and a leather satchel was slung over a shoulder. Gripped in one hand, at the ready, was a strange looking knife made of a dull-white material. I realized it was bone.

Another word appeared below this image of me: *Tracker*.

What, by the stars, was going on?

More words appeared.

Tracker

This class grants a character the ability to traverse the many dangerous realms of carnage with ease. Skilled in hunting and skinning, a tracker can find prey in the most difficult of terrain. At later levels, trackers can learn to capture and train various beasts and creatures (non-humanoid).

+2 Reflex Attribute

+5 Power

+10% Skinning skill

+5% Tracking skill

Accept this character – Yes / No?

If I could blink in confusion, I would have. What was this? For a few moments I could only stare in bewilderment at the feral version of myself. Had I accidentally entered one of the sims in the ship's database?

Then I recalled the words from before: Joining Server.

What if I could get out of this somehow? I tried to say no, but still couldn't speak. Then I noticed the word Yes was highlighted. I focused on the word No, hoping that would pull me out.

The No highlighted and flashed once. Then the image of me quickly slid out of view and vanished. It was replaced by another version of me, this one different than before.

This one was covered from head to toe in clothing made from a patchwork of material. Skin, I realized with horror. Human skin. A necklace of severed ears hung from her neck. Her head was shaved bald, and a strange tattooed symbol covered her scalp. Her eyes weren't as wild and feral as the tracker, but were no less menacing.

Several packs were strapped to her back at odd angles, each made of hide. Across her waist was a cord-like belt which hung with several little pouches, each with a symbol stitched onto them.

She gripped an object in a clenched fist, and long wicked teeth stuck out between her fingers. A piece of an animal's jawbone.

This one had an oddly fitting name to go with its appearance.

Gore Fiend

This class grants the character the ability to salvage better materials for crafting. In tune with an enemy's weaknesses, a gore fiend can increase the chances of making a quicker kill. One of the few classes to be allowed to practice Death magic at later levels.

+2 Mind Attribute

+10% roll bonus when claiming an Enhanced Item.

+5% Critical Hit Chance

Immune to Blood Madness (A Death magic penalty)

Accept this character – Yes / No?

My frustration grew. I hadn't been dropped from this bizarre selection screen, and appeared to be stuck. What was this nonsense? Where was Otto?

Trying to keep my growing anger in check I selected no. Then no again, and again. Rapidly, various classes zipped past, each a snapshot of me in some macabre state of dress; Demon Dancer, Plains Warrior, Shadow Rogue, Cloud Mage, Dream Champion, Festered, The Unknown, Sorcerer, Giant Whisperer, Feral One, Glacial Knight, Bone Templar. And still it went on. Dozens and dozens of them.

Finally, I got the hint. No wasn't the answer to escaping my purgatory of this bizarre menu. I stopped selecting no and the screen halted on a class. Not caring what it was, I selected Yes.

To my relief, the screen changed, but not before catching a glimpse of the class name I'd selected.

Berserker.

The torches vanished and my view angled upwards to face the roiling black clouds. From deep within their depths flashed yellow and purple lights, indicating something sinister beyond.

Another selection screen appeared, and I moaned inwardly with annoyance.

Choose a God:

This time, instead of an image of me in a grizzly outfit, a reddish symbol filled my view. It was hard to discern and I didn't care to interpret its meaning – a red lake channeling over a cliff, forming a waterfall of red?

This was followed by more words.

Blood God

Slain in the Third Great War, the Blood God seeks a return to the mortal plain and revenge on those gods who betrayed him. With you by his side the Blood God would destroy his enemies and subjugate all who-."

Don't care! I wanted to shout. I ignored the rest of story telling gibberish and scanned downward. Pages of nonsense scrolled up until it stopped at what I was looking for. A selection.

Bind yourself to this God – Yes / No?

Yes.

Are you certain of this choice? Binding yourself to a God defines your main quest path, as well as effecting unlockable talents-.

I ignored the rest and went straight to the confirmation. Yes. This is my damned selection. Get me out of this mess!

You are bound to the Blood God. There is no hope for your soul.

If I could have laughed, I would have. Whoever came up with this garbage should be demoted or fired, or whatever happened to washed up sim creators.

All messages vanished and only the angry clouds remained. After several seconds I feared I'd be stuck like this, but soon the clouds parted. Beyond them was the strange yellow and purple lights.

When the clouds rolled out of view I realized I was moving. Without warning, my hands appeared before me. What little elation I felt was negated when an overwhelming sense of suffocation pressed down upon my chest.

My hands flailed and hit something solid. The strange yellow and purple light had moved. They weren't lights, but some kind of barrier.

I gagged and something red sloshed across my vision. Realizing I finally had a body again, I looked around.

A sticky red liquid splashed around my head, and I sensed I was laying down in a pool of the stuff. Confused, I tried to sit up, but my forehead butted against the barrier which stretched.

Where was I?

Confused, I noticed the red liquid was rising. I pressed my face up against the barrier, keeping my mouth above, but I accidentally took a big swallow.

Coppery. Salty.

Blood.

Gagging, I screamed in horror, the sudden sound of my voice after the long silence was almost deafening within the constrictive confines of my prison.

Panicked, I slashed upwards and was surprised when my hand punched through the barrier. Desperate, I used both hands to rip and tear at the hole I'd created. In seconds, I managed to make it big enough to sit up.

Blood in my eyes blurred my vision, but I sensed a ledge next to me. I flung my body to the side and was relieved when my torso smacked down on a hard surface.

Still screaming and shrieking, I clamored through the barrier and out of the bloody pool. Safe for the moment, I curled over on my knees and retched my guts out. Copious amounts of thick red blood splattered the ground.

When there was no more to vomit, I slumped to my side, clutching my stomach with both arms. By the stars, what had just happened?

After several moments of gasping, I rubbed the sticky blood from my eyes.

Beside me was a long, narrow trough in the ground, like a grave. Thick blood filled it to its edge. Stretched taught across its surface was the barrier which I'd torn down the middle.

A membrane.

I'd been in that? My mind reeled, aghast.

I glanced around. I was laying on hard ground, surrounded by piles of boulders and rocks. Above was open sky. Dark clouds swirled past, the same clouds I'd seen at the selection screen.

From behind, a voice spoke, startling me.

"It would appear the Blood God has summoned to me a new candidate."

CHAPTER THREE

I turned around and looked up.

A man stood over me. Even from this angle I could see he was short. His head was bald and glinted with a sheen of sweat. He wore a blood-red leather vest which exposed his flabby arms and did little to conceal a wide protruding gut. A swath of dark leather wrapped around his waist and hung down to his scarred knees.

In one plump hand he held a staff. No, not a staff; a spinal column topped with an engraved human skull.

Stunned, I could only stare at this grotesque apparition for several moments.

The man's frog-like countenance scowled down at me. "Are you mute, bitch? Say something!"

I blinked at him, still trying to recover from what just happened. First I was on my ship, then we suffered some kind of attack, then I was assailed by images, followed by nearly drowning in a pit of blood. Safe to assume I wasn't at my best in that very moment, but I did manage to speak. "Where am I? What's happening?"

Unimpressed, the man's scowl deepened forming fat ripples up his forehead. "At least you're not another still-born. What is your name, woman?"

Words appeared before me, and the world seemed to slow down to a crawl.

Character's name?

I grunted with annoyance. "I don't have time for this. Get me out of here!"

Nothing happened. The message remained.

Frustrated, I said, "I wish to log out now. Please!" I figured I'd accidentally got thrown into a sim. Is that what happened? The ship was damaged and I'd somehow interfaced with a sim while trying to access systems?

Again, nothing changed. When I tried to move, I found my body was immobile, frozen in place.

Fine. If I needed to go through the motions, I would. "Okay. My name is Zyra. Got that?"

Character's name Zyra.

The message vanished and the world resumed again.

The man's scowl lessened, but only a little. "Zyra. A good name. A strong name. One that will strike fear in our enemies!" A wide reptilian smile broke across his face, revealing angular, yellow teeth.

Happy to get that out of the way, I stood only to realize I was completely naked, save for a narrow loincloth fitted tightly around my waist. I fought back the impulse to try and cover myself, but I was too annoyed to care. Besides, this was just a sim. "I want to log off. How do I do that?"

The scowl returned. "You speak too much, woman. There is no time for your prattle. The Blood God has tasks for you to perform. You must prove yourself worthy to him!"

Talking to him wasn't going to work. I looked about searching for an access screen. Most sims kept one near during play so you could access the sim's program in case verbal cues didn't work.

I stood in a wide clearing among stone piles. A path between them appeared to be the only exist, short of climbing. In the center was the disgusting pool of blood. On the other side was a tall white crystal, like a pillar, which glowed softly.

Confused, I said, "Where is the nearest access panel?" As a construct of the sim, he had to answer.

"What gibberish do you speak?" said the vile-looking fat man. "There is nothing for you except service to the Blood God. But first I must make an assessment of you. Even as a selected candidate you must meet basic requirements."

Wanting nothing more to do with him, I turned away. Maybe if I touched one of the rocks or the crystal pillar the panel would appear. But when I tried to move I found my legs rooted to the ground.

"By the stars! What is this?" I said, my temper growing. "Let me go. I need to move."

The man shook his head, his many chins jiggling with agitation. "You need to shut up while I look you over. Here, now. What can we make of you?"

A floating status screen appeared before me.

Name: Zyra

Class: Berserker

Level: 1 (500 Blood Points for Level 2)

Talent Points: 1 (1 Unused)

Blood Points: 0

Health Points: 50

Magic Points: 20

Power: 25

Might: 12 (+2 Class Bonus)

Reflex: 10

Mind: 10

Vigor: 12 (+2 Class Bonus)

Deity: Blood God. (+10% Bonus Blood Points Earned)

Marks: None

Skills:

Butchery: 5% (+1 Weapon Damage)

Hand-to-hand: 5% (+1 Unarmed Damage)

"Hmm," the man said as he looked over the screen from the other side. "A berserker. I see you already have Butchery and Hand-to-hand skills. Those will most certainly be used. Our god craves savagery in his followers. You will be no exception."

Now angry beyond words, I shouted at him, the screen vanishing. "This has gone on long enough! My ship needs me, damnit! Log me off, or get me access to the bridge systems or something!" Looking up at the bleak clouds and screamed up at them. "Otto! Otto! What, by the bloody stars, is going on? Sitrep!"

The man watched me rant and rave, then nodded. "Anger is good. Yes. Anger gets one's blood lust up. Aids in the slaughter. This I can work with."

"Oh, for the love of..." I shouted. "Get me out of here!" I was beside myself with rage. I needed out of this sim!

"Out?" the man said, arching a hairless brow. "There is no out once you have given yourself over to the Blood God. Your soul is his now. For now and all eternity. But fear not, bitch. You time in this realm will not be wasted. Our god needs his weapons for the coming war. And use you he will."

My temper fueled haze cleared slightly as I attempted get a hold of myself. The Captain's Protocol!

To the man and the dark world around me, I shouted, "Captain's Protocol! One Alpha Nine Nine Gamma Six!" The protocol allowed to override any system at any time on the ship, regardless of the situation. One of the perks of being the captain. I'd been too overwhelmed with this fantasy horrorland to think of it, at first. If anything, it would immediately bring a halt to this program or at least allow me to finally access the ship's systems.

This time, both of the man's hairless brows crawled up his face. "What is this? Are you attempting to invoke an ability? You've just arrived, you daft cow. You haven't harvested any Marks to use! Ha!"

Nothing happened, and I cursed. Were the ship's systems so damaged I was trapped? Sims were a favorite pastime for deep space explorers. Immersed in another world allowed travelers the luxury of occupying themselves when not in hibernation. They'd also advanced far enough that you no longer needed to wear visors or masks, or any other type of interface. Simply select the sim, and sit back and relax.

Somehow, I'd logged into this sim and was beginning to suspect it may have been Otto's doing. He controlled everything. Perhaps it was to protect my mind from the harsh reality of the ship cracking open. The same technology used for sims was also used to induce patients before surgery. I envisioned my limp body sprawled on the deck of the bridge, eyes rolled back in my head, the connection to the damaged computer systems tenuous.

But that, too, didn't make much sense. I knew the ship had been attacked. I heard the tearing of the ship's hull. I should be dead. We should all be dead.

I sudden slap across the face jolted me out of my thoughts. Temper flaring, I glared at the ugly man.

"I have your attention, now, do I?" he said, stepping back. "Good. Then we can begin."

"You stupid son of a..." I started to shout when a terrifying realization overcame me.

He *hit* me. Actual physical contact. And I felt it. Pain. Sims couldn't do that.

A cold pang of fear pierced my chest. What kind of sim was this?

Worried now, I asked, "What is the name of this simulation?"

"Simulation?" the man said, confused. "What is a simulation? A form of magic?"

Uh oh. Every sim in existence happily gave you its name and details when asking non-player characters. Basic information was always available, regardless if it broke immersion. But it appeared I couldn't access it now, if it was available at all.

I decided on a different approach. "What is your name?"

"My name is Chak!" he said, slapping himself on the belly with pride. "I am a priest in the order of the Blood God! May his hunger never end!"

A information screen appeared above him, attaching itself to his head.

Chak – Blood Priest / Guide
Health 100%
Magic 100%
Bound to the Blood God

The health had a red bar next to it, the magic, blue.

I chose my next words carefully. "Chak, thank you for your help. But I am tired and wish to pause my journey. Is there a place to rest for a while?" Sleeping in a sim always brought you out of it. I hoped this one was no different.

Chak's scowl returned. "Rest? Why, you've only just been created." He pointed at the bloody trough next to me. "Pulled yourself out of the Blood God's womb. There is no rest now. Only training."

Womb? I looked down at the hole, revolted. There had to be a way to log out. Maybe it wasn't by sleeping.

Chak tapped his gruesome staff on the ground to get my attention. "Enough prattle. You have your level one talent point to assign. Pull up your talent trees."

"Talent trees?" I said, my mind distracted with worry.

Another floating screen appeared, this one with three tabs along the bottom: Offensive, Defensive, Passive. The Offensive one was open showing a small symbol of a red fist at its bottom. Looking at the symbol brought up its information.

Bash 0/3
Cost: 5 Power
Cooldown: 2 minutes
This allows the user to Bash an opponent with greater strength, causing extra damage and the chance to disorient them.
+35% to Hit
+35% Damage
+15% Chance to Stun for 2 seconds

"Place your point into it," Chak said.

I saw another floating line.

Unused Talent Points: 1

No, I didn't want to place anything anywhere, other than my foot up this guy's ass. But I felt the need to do as he asked if to just get rid of the screen.

Instinctively, I pointed a blood-crusted finger at the Bash symbol. It changed from 0/3 to 1/3.

Words appeared in a small box at the bottom left of my vision.

You have learned the Bash ability.

The talent-tree screen vanished.

"Excellent! Each time you purchase a level with blood points, you earn a talent point. Placing talent points into known abilities increases their power, while putting a point into unknown abilities allows you to learn them."

"Uh huh," I said, uninterested. I looked over the drying blood covering my body. How was I going to wash this stuff off?

"And now to earn those precious blood points," Chak said with an oily grin, "with your first kill!"

Without warning, my frozen legs became unstuck, nearly causing me to pitch over into the blood pool. Surprised, I moved my legs around, and stretched them out.

"It is now I shall give you your first quest," Chak said. "You are to slay an enemy of the Blo-."

I startled him by walking past and toward the path leading out.

"What are you doing?" he called after me. "You need to accept the quest first!"

"Don't care!" I said over my shoulder. If this toad couldn't show me how to exit this sim, someone else might.

"Stop!" he shouted, but I ignored him.

I crossed the threshold of the clearing and into the path, jumbled rocks piled high on each side. It led away a few dozen paces and turned right. But before I could take another step, a jagged row of wooden spikes suddenly jutted out from the ground ahead, causing me to jump back. They extended upwards and stopped, forming a high wall, blocking the path completely.

Oh, of course, I thought.

I spun around to yell at Chek. "Take this down now or I'll-."

My words ended in a scream of pain.

Chak had rushed up behind me and tapped me on the hip with the skull at the end of the staff. It was a gentle motion, one that you wouldn't think could hurt. But it did.

An intense burning sensation blossomed where I'd been touched, and spread quickly. The pain was horrific.

I backed up, desperate to get away from him, but he only stood and watched me. Looking down at my hip, I could see the flesh was boiling away exposing the bone beneath.

You have taken 5 health points of acid damage!

You have taken 5 health points of acid damage!

More messages scrolled up at the bottom left of my vision, but I didn't care. Shocked and convulsing with pain, I fell to the ground. I screamed and screamed as it spread over my body, eating my flesh and bones.

Chak stood over me, impassive; a petulant look on his face.

Through the blinding agony I witnessed my chest dissolve, feeling every bit of it go. My rib cage went, then my internal organs, until my beating heart was exposed. And I watched it all, helpless. At some point I went mad. Well and truly mad.

When the acid finally reached my rapidly beating heart, it imploded inward, blood gushing within the exposed cavity of my chest.

In the final moments, Chak leaned close and said, "Now maybe you will listen to me, bitch."

You have taken 5 health points of acid damage!

You have 0 health points.

As I gasped my final breath, huge words loomed before me.

You have died.

Then, whiteness.

CHAPTER FOUR

Again, whiteness.

The moment the words of my death appeared, the pain mercifully ceased. Relieved, I let the peace of the white space fill my soul. I had never experienced pain like that before. Nothing even close.

I'd broken my wrist once after a fall. One of my earliest survey missions was in a small shuttle-jumper called a Bumblebee. Only capable of impulse travel, it was used to visit moons or large asteroids from a station. My team landed on a tiny moon, and I felt the compulsion to climb the walls of a nearby crater. Although the gravity was low, I was colossally clumsy, and landed wrong when I slipped.

That hurt a lot. But whatever Chak did to me, touching me with the staff, was a pain a thousand times more agonizing than a broken wrist. A million times worse.

No sim would do that to a participant. No sim could. Some of the best ones could simulate some form of touch, but only if you wore a full body suit. The ones we used on the Corena only stimulated through the eyes. You have a faint sense of touch, but you never felt anything truly solid. Or pain.

This sim did it all. Things had mass. The blood tasted like blood. The scorching pain of flesh being dissolved. No, this wasn't a ship sim.

Before I could contemplate it further, the whiteness started to fade. A familiar yellow and purple design formed before me. Suddenly, blood sloshed into my ears and spattered my face.

I was back in another bloody grave.

Although I was aware of where I was this time, I still had to fight back the primal urge to panic.

I scratched and punched at the membrane above me, my body twisting and turning in the deep blood. Finally, I punched through and the sight of dark clouds high above filled my vision.

I pulled myself out of the pool and flopped onto the ground, tired from the effort.

As I wiped blood from face to keep it from getting in my eyes, a man stood above me. Chak.

"Care to try, again?" he said. A grin tugged at the edges of his oily lips.

Gasping for air, I said, "Why did you do that?" My eyes went to the skull on the end of his staff. It grinned at me.

Chak harrumphed. "Why? Because you asked me to. Begged me. With your insolence, and your disdain for the god whom you serve."

Carefully, with one eye on the staff, I got to my feet. Looking over my body I could see I was the same as before. Naked, save for a tiny loincloth, and drenched in sticky blood.

The blood priest grinned at my fearful expression. "There are two absolutes in this world, woman. Blood and pain. And you've managed to indulge both in your short time here." He leaned close, grinning. "I envy you."

There was no way I wanted to be touched by that staff again. None. So whatever this fat tub of grease wanted me to do, I'd do it.

"Can I ask a question?" I said, genuinely fearful.

Chak nodded. "Yes, of course. Not only am I your disciplinarian, I am also your guide, at least until you are ready."

"What is this place?" I figured the direct approach might get me somewhere.

He titled his chin up in thought. For a brief moment, I was afraid he might touch me with the staff. Then he said, "You don't know? How can you not?"

"I'm new here," I said and flinched as a flashing cascade of lightning spidered through the clouds above. "I don't understand what is going on, why I'm here."

The fat man watched me for a few moments before he spoke. "Hmmm. That is interesting you would ask these things. It has been a long, long time since anyone had been picked as a candidate, and even then they weren't as ignorant as you." His fingers holding his staff flexed slightly.

Alarmed, I quickly said, "If I am to serve the, uh, Blood God, I need to understand. Only then can I do what is needed of me." Play along. It was my only option at the moment.

Chak watched me, taking some kind of measure. He said, "Yes. Very well. If only to help speed things along, I will tell you." He raised hands in the air, flabby arms jiggling. "This is the Realm of Carnage. It is here that the gods do battle with one another. A vast battleground. One that has suffered eons of conflict and strife as a result."

He waved a hand around the clearing. "We stand within a blight upon the Realm, a chasm from which the Blood God shall rise, again."

"Rise?" I said.

"Yes. Our god was betrayed. Slain in battle by those whom he thought of as allies. His death brought a great pain upon the world. But with your help, he shall return and gain his revenge!" His eyes grew wide, almost feverish.

I kept my face neutral. It sounded goofy enough to be a sim world, but at a hyper-level of realism I wasn't keen on.

"And my purpose for being here?" I asked.

Chak snorted in derision. "Purpose? Your purpose is the same as mine – to serve the Blood God. We are not only his acolytes in the Realm, we are also his weapons he needs to fight his enemies." He pointed at me. "You are one of those weapons. If you do as he commands, perhaps you could be his greatest champion. But first, you must be tested."

"Okay, what is required of me?"

The fat man smiled, his cheeks plump and rubbery. "Ah, that is what I want to hear. You are to kill an enemy of the Blood God. This chasm is filled with them, all in service to craven gods who seek to impede his return." He pointed his finger at the wooden gate. It retracted back into the ground revealing the path beyond.

You have been given a quest: First Kill
Find and slay two Burned Men who skulk nearby.
Reward: 200 Blood Points

I blinked at the task. "You want me to kill them?"

For the first time, Chak laughed, fat rolls heaving. When he finished, he said, "Woman, it is your main point for existing at all. Yes, kill them. And after, there will be more to kill. And after them, even more! Legions! Hordes! You will slay so many the empty oceans of Quddin could not be able to contain their corpses!"

Okay, then. I turned and walked out of the clearing and past the gate. Struck with I thought, I stopped and asked, "Don't I need a weapon?"

Chak looked at me, eyes gleaming. "You are the weapon." He waved his hand and the gate slide up from the ground, blocking me from the clearing.

Well, at least I didn't have to talk to him. Hands on my hips, I looked around. The stacks of ragged stone formed walls on either side, creating a path that turned to the right. Looking above them, I could see a distance cliff face that stretched off into the distance. Above, the clouds twisted and turned like a blackened ocean caught in a storm, punctuated by pulses of lightning.

You are the weapon. That didn't sound good.

Worried idling at the gate might instigate another acid attack, I moved away and down the path. The hard ground was coarse and warm beneath my bare feet. I tried scraping the drying blood off my skin, but only made it appear worse. How I longed for the shower tube back on the ship.

The Corena.

Where was she? It had been my home for close to three years and countless surveys. The sound of its hull cracking rang through my ears, a sound no captain wanted to hear. The sound of death. Yet, I was alive, so that meant it had to have survived, too, right? I wouldn't be here in this place if the ship had been destroyed. But what of its fate? And my crew? I could only speculate as to what happened to them. Until I can find those answers, I'd play along with this crazy game.

The path led several dozens paces away from the gate and then turned sharply to the left. As I approached, I heard something ahead. I stopped to listen. The sound came again, from around the turn. Voices. They were low, almost guttural. Two men talking.

Carefully, I approached the edge of the wall, keeping my body pressed against it, then slowly peeked.

The path led into a wider area, another clearing. Two men where here, sitting on the ground, facing each other. A woman lay between them. She was on her stomach, her face turned toward me. For a brief moment I feared she would spot me and raise an alarm. But her eyes told me that wouldn't happen. She was dead.

"Ain't respectful, that's all I say," one man said, his voice echoing off the rocky walls. He was bald headed and naked, save for a loincloth.

"Respect has nothing to do with it," the other man said. He was nearly naked, too, only his bald scalp was crested by a thin hedge of hair forming a mohawk. "If it ain't tradable, it ain't tradable. Them's the rules."

Neither looked in my direction, lost in their conversation. But it wasn't what they were saying which held my interest, it was their skin.

Every inch of their bodies was covered in a flaky black soot, as if their flesh had been scorched in a fire. It looked incredibly painful, yet neither seemed to mind. Instead, they focused on what they were doing.

The first man shrugged. "Well, I now them's the rules. Don't mean I have to like it. I can't be hauling goods all the way to the trader only to be told my hard gotten gains ain't worth a dead slave's ass. Just frustrating, is all." He raised something to his mouth and bit into it, gnashing it with yellowed teeth.

"Well, you may not have been able to trade for proper food, but at least we found this one to eat," Mohawk said, chuckling. He bit into something, too.

I then realized what they were doing – they were eating the woman.

I nearly retched in revulsion as the two dined with gusto, tearing at the slabs of raw pink flesh in their hands. These were the two I was expected to kill?

Little information markers sprung up above their heads, both identical.

Burned Man
Health: 100%
Magic: 100%
Bound to the Molten God

The woman had one too which simply said Corpse of Slave.

Okay, this was it then, I thought as the two enjoyed their meal. But how was I expected to fight them, let alone kill them? Looking around for a weapon of some kind, I found a fist sized rock and picked it up.

Hefting it in my hand, I glared at the men. Now what? Throw it? It was possible I could hit one, but it might not be enough. I'd never been in a fight before in my life. Not even in school. Sure, I grappled during the physical training at the academy, but that was mostly for exercise.

I had no fighting experience of any kind. And I could only guess as to how to actually kill someone. Doubt crept into the back of my mind and I hesitated.

Mohawk took a big swallow. "Well, this beats skagg meat any day, if you know what I mean?"

The other laughed, bits of flesh spraying from his mouth. "Ha! Ain't that the truth of it. Expect us to scurry around here in the chasm on a fool's errand without a proper meal, then we'll eat any slave we find. Traders be damned!"

Both men laughed. My gaze fell upon the poor dead woman, naked with wide red strips cut from her back. I felt angry.

I might not have any experience fighting, but I did have something. The element of surprise.

Waiting until they both hunched over to take another bite, I quickly rounded the corner and launched myself across the clearing. The slapping of my feet on the ground betrayed my attempt to keep silent and I feared they'd hear me before I reached them.

Turned out, luck was on my side.

I sprinted across the short distance to where they sat so fast, they didn't notice me until I was on top of them.

Baldy saw me first, turning his head toward me, mouth full of flesh.

With my running momentum unchecked, I swung the rock in my hand and cracked it across the back of his skull. A grim, yet satisfying crunch let me know I'd hit home.

You hit the Burned Man for 10 health points of blunt damage!

Baldy keeled over onto his side, screaming in pain, no longer interested in his snack.

Mohawk scrambled to his feet, wide-eyed in surprise. Hanging from his waist was what appeared to be a club of some kind. He dropped the woman's cut flesh and grabbed the club, shaking it menacingly.

We stood facing one another, my bloody rock held over my shoulder, his club several inches from my face.

The shock wearing off, Mohawk glanced down at his friend who was convulsing on the ground. Then he looked me over, sizing me up.

My heart thudded in my chest. Why couldn't I just attack him while I still had the advantage? Fighting wasn't natural to me, like a strange alien dance. Had I been more skilled in its nuances, I would have jumped on him. But I hesitated.

Mohawk met my gaze, and said, "I know what you are."

"Don't you dare call me a bitch," I said.

"A berserker." His voice had an edge of reverence to it, almost awe.

I couldn't hold back any longer, and leapt forward. Lacking anything to block the club, I tried to grab onto it with my free hand while striking down with the rock.

But Mohawk's momentary paralysis evaporated the second I moved, and quickly stepped back out of reach. As I swung downward with the rock, he pulled the club to one side and hit me in the face with it.

You have been hit for 4 health points of blunt damage!

Stars danced across my vision, and my knees buckled. As I staggered, Mohawk shouted with glee and brought the club down on my back. Somehow, I pulled away and the club only glanced off my shoulder. The downward force of the blow still dropped me to one knee, and for a moment I couldn't breath.

You have been hit for 5 health points of blunt damage!

Mohawk stood over me and snickered. "Dumb bitch. Dumb, stupid bitch berserker. I thought your kind were dangerous. Guess not, huh?"

I tried to speak, but couldn't. Was my jaw broken?

He reveled in the moment. "Never had a berserker before. Think I'll finally get to enjoy one after all. Once one way, then another. Fun then feast."

My double vision faded and I turned my head to look up at him.

He said, "Yeah, you know what's coming. Just like this slave did. Only I'm going to take my time with you. Gods be damned, you look good enough to eat!" He raised the club high over his head with both hands.

When I first sprinted into the clearing I'd completely forgotten about my new ability. In my haste to get away from Chak I barely gave it any thought.

Now I did.

As Mohawk raised the club, a shout of victory on his lips, I gripped the rock with both hands and drove it into his groin with all my strength.

Use Bash Ability.

It was like punching through a bag of laundry. I felt my hands crush his gut and hit the pelvis bone on the other side.

Mohawk's victory shout came out a hoarse gasp as his innards ruptured.

I was only partially aware that a small timer appeared at the corner of my vision, but I ignored it. As Mohawk crumpled to the ground, I brought the rock down against his temple. Another satisfying crunch. This was accompanied by a mewling noise from Mohawk's mouth, so I brought the rock down, again, to shut him up. It worked. I hit him, again and again.

"Fun then feast!" I screeched at the top of my lungs, punctuating the words with the rock. "Fun then feast!"

I only stopped once I realized there was no longer a face to scream at. Tired, I slid off the dead man's corpse, panting. My face hurt terribly and my left shoulder was completely numb. I coughed up some blood. Had I fractured a rib and punctured a lung? He hit me hard enough.

As I sat slouched over, contemplating my pains, Baldy moaned.

Damn. And here I thought I was done.

I noticed my rock was missing. Looking around I couldn't find where I'd dropped it. My eyes snagged on the club which Mohawk still held in his death grip. His hand was twitching slightly, as if to the beat of some far off music.

Baldy moaned again, this time moving a little, as if coming to.

I grabbed the club by the handle and wrestled it out of the dead man's grip.

You have taken an item: Simple Bone Club

Durability: Usable

Damage: 1-6

Tradable

I ignored the message and moved to Baldy, stumbling a little. That hit to the face really did a number on me.

Baldy had pulled himself up to his knees, a piece of brain poking out of the collapsed hole at the back of his head. He swayed back and forth, ready to fall over.

Raising the club up, I paused long enough to say, "Fun then feast!"

Baldy launched into me. His attack was so sudden, the club was wrenched from my grasp.

I landed hard on my back and cracked my head on the ground. Somewhere I heard someone gurgling, then realized it was me. Baldy was laying on top of me, hands around my throat. The burned flesh of his face contorted with rage, our noses touching.

I struggled to push him off, but he was too strong and heavy. My hands batted at his sides, fingernails tearing at his flesh, but nothing altered the intensity of his attack. I couldn't breathe. I was going to die. Again.

My right hand found something, fist-sized and hard. With a choking grunt, I swung the rock at his head. He must have sensed the movement because he turned to look, allowing the rock to hit his left eye. The impact smashed it like a grape and his head titled back letting me shove him off.

On his back, clutching at his face, he wailed and whimpered in pain.

Quickly I straddled his chest, pinning him down. I brought the rock down on his head, again and again, but this time too tired to chant.

After he finally went still, I slid off of him.

A message appeared.

Quest completed: First Kill

You have slain both Burned Men. Return to Chak for your next task.

Reward: 200 Blood Points

Doubled over on the ground, I coughed and wretched, trying to regain the ability to breathe again. It took several long minutes before I could roll on my back and stare up at the streaming carpet of clouds.

By the stars, I hurt! But I'd done it. I killed two men.

I have no idea how long I lay there, but it was long enough for me to start to doze, the numbing pain over my body acting like a warm blanket. A sudden noise pulled me from the brink of sleep, and I struggled to raise myself up on my elbows.

Worried the dead men might have some more surprises, I looked them over. They were still. Just as dead as the poor slave girl. She looked so young.

That noise again, this time coming from beyond the rocky wall to my left. A hiss followed by scraping. Suddenly, two yellowish eyes appeared within the murk above the wall. Something was climbing over it.

Scaled claws gripped the top edge of the wall, and a long serpent-like tongue slithered out of the darkness beneath the eyes to caress the air.

I didn't need any more coaxing. Grunting with effort, I pulled myself up the closest wall to my feet. Tearing my gaze away from the monstrous thing sliding down into the clearing at the other side, I barely had the presence of mind to scoop up the club.

Then, without a look back, I half-staggered, half-fell into the pathway I'd entered from. As I rounded the bend and careened off a wall, I hurried away. All the while trying to ignore the wet sound of something feasting behind me.

CHAPTER FIVE

I stumbled along the path, using the rock walls to keep me upright and moving. Each time I coughed, the blood I spat out became thicker.

That was not what I had expected for a fight. Short and brutal. But I'd won, miraculously.

Several messages sat unread in the message box at the corner of my vision. I'd been too busy fighting for my life to notice them.

You have slain a Burned Man. You have gained 150 Blood Points. Spend them wisely.

You have slain a Burned Man. You have gained 150 Blood Points. Spend them wisely.

Bash cooldown has expired. Ability available.

The last message must have coincided with the little timer I saw after punching Mohawk through the guts. Glancing at the ability's description showed the timer was for two minutes. I'd just learned that two minutes is a long time to wait when in combat.

I examined the club in my hand. It was certainly of bone, but oddly shaped. As if smaller bones had been fused together and molded in a more ergonomic and lethal shape. A tiny fleck of blood on its heavier end blemished its eggshell color. My blood.

Finally, I reached the end of the path and the gateway beyond. But a savage coughing fit sent me to my knees. It was then I noticed a thin red bar along the right side of my vision. *Health 8%.*

Wonderful.

Movement caught my eye, and for a moment, I feared the thing back at the clearing at somehow cut me off. But it was Chak, emerging through the gate.

"Ah, she has returned. Successful, I hope?" he said. He stood a short distance away, staff in hand.

"Yup," I said, blood frothing at my lips with the word. "If nearly getting beaten to death counts as success."

This made Chak laugh, boisterously. "Ha! And a sense of humor, too, even through all that pain. Did you forget what I told you? Blood and pain. Embrace them. It will make your journey easier."

"If you say so," I said, and slumped against the rock wall. The movement made me scream in pain, and I clutched at my side.

"Internal injuries," Chak said, making a tsk-tsk noise. "Those are the worst. And to think, this is but a small taste of the exquisite banquet of agony you will dine upon in the future."

Wow, he really knew how to make it sound appealing. "Can I get a little help here?" I was pretty certain I was bleeding internally. My Health bar suddenly dropped to 5%.

"Help? Why, yes I *could* help you." He stood immobile, grinning that oily grin.

What did he want me to do? "Please?" More frothy blood, this time through my nose.

"Come to me," he said, watching intently.

For a second I thought he might be joking, but his expression told otherwise.

The pain was blinding. "But I..."

"Crawl," he said. "Bitch."

I wanted to tell him off. I wanted to scream at him. Tell him never to call me that again. But I didn't.

I crawled. Using my one good arm, I dragged myself across the ground, the rock beneath scraping my skin.

Health 3%.

Chak waited.

What was this guy's problem? I pulled myself along, until I collapsed at his feet and rolled onto my back.

Health 2%.

Staring down at me, Chak said, "Never forget who I am. Your disciplinarian, your guide..."

Health 1%.

A familiar whiteness played around the edges of my vision. Here we go again, I thought through the painful haze.

Chak leaned down and painfully grabbed one of my breasts. "And your savior!"

Suddenly, my pain began to subside. Little by little it faded. Messages were scrolling up in the corner.

Chak has healed you for 5 Health Points.

Chak has healed you for 5 Health Points.

I felt the odd sensation of my ribs snapping into place, my lung becoming whole and drained of blood. My jaw reset itself, and the numbness in my shoulder vanished.

It took roughly a minute, after which I felt incredible and my health bar showed it. *Health 100%.*

By the stars, that felt great!

I realized I was still on my back, looking up at the sweaty fat man holding my breast. Not certain what to say, I sat up. As I did, Chak gave one last painful squeeze and let go.

As I stood, he glared at me, as if daring me to say something. I didn't.

At least, not now.

"Thank you," I forced myself to say.

"I am not the one to thank. The Blood God is the one whom you owe all your gratitude."

"Okay," I said, not sure how to follow that up. I looked over my naked form. It was still crusted with the blood from the pool, but also my own, and the men I'd killed. But other than that, I was whole again. "That's a good trick. How did you do it?" And how can I do it, too?

Chak snorted. "You are jumping ahead. We were going to cover Marks a little later. But since you brought it up." He pulled back one of the flaps of his odd vest, exposing his sagging left bicep. He had far bigger breasts than me.

Across his collarbone and over his shoulder was a tattoo. It was archaic, with odd symbols and images of which I couldn't identify.

"A tattoo?" I said, hoping he'd just cover himself up.

"A Mark," he said. "*Look* at it."

I focused on the tattoo and, suddenly, an information screen appeared next to it.

Mark of Healing

This Mark grants the wearer the ability to recover health points for themselves, or others via touch.

Maximum 5 health points every 5 seconds.

Cost: 10 Blood Points per health point.

"Whoa," I said. "That is a nice trick. Where can I buy one of those?"

"You do not buy Marks," Chak said, covering it again. "You earn them in battle. But we will get to that soon enough." He waved to the gate. "Come."

I followed him back into the little clearing.

Chak said, "Tell me, how many Blood Points do you have?"

"I dunno," I blurted without thinking. When he scowled I said, "Really, I don't. I got a bunch when I killed those two."

"Check your statistics," Chak drawled, annoyed.

"How do I..." I started to say when it appeared before me. Apparently, I just needed to think of it.

Blood Points: 500

Chak said, "Now, look at your level."

"One," I said. Then I noticed the words next to it. *500 Blood Points for Level 2.*

"You now have the points required to purchase your next level," Chak said, "if you wanted to."

"Don't I want to?"

Chak held up a chubby finger. "Blood Points are gained by slaying opponents. Although legion, the enemies of the Blood God may not give you many points, so you must hoard them and spend them wisely."

"On levels?"

"Levels, yes, but also for other things."

His Mark healed at the cost of 10 Blood Points per health point. I couldn't tell if that was cheap or not.

Chak said, "You must also use Blood Points to craft items, like weapons and armor. But you will learn of those, too. Simply remember this: All things have a price in this Realm, and the currency is death."

Charming. I was beginning to believe this sim would be better suited for teenage boys rather than a middle aged female surveyor.

I tried not to yawn. "So you want me to spend these points?"

He nodded.

I was about to ask how when a message appeared. Thought induced, no doubt.

Purchase Level 2 for 500 Blood Points?

"Yes, do it," I said.

Purchased. You are now at level 2. You have gained 1 talent point and 2 attribute points.

When I told Chak, he nodded. "Now, bring up your talent tree."

I did and looked at the Bash ability.

Bash 1/3

Next point gives:

Cost: 7 Power

Cooldown: 1 minute 45 seconds

This allows the user to Bash an opponent with greater force, causing greater damage and the chance to disorient them.

+40% to Hit

+40% Damage

+25% to Stun for 4 seconds

"Another point will boost its power," I said. It looked straightforward enough.

"Correct, but don't assign it just yet. Look at your Defensive tab."

The talent-tree switched over to the Defensive tab. A single icon sat at the bottom, but was grayed out.

Devil's Dance 0/5

Cost: 10 Power

Cooldown: 10 minutes

This allows the user to dodge all physical attacks with 100% success for a duration of 5 seconds.

"Cool," I said. Now that would be handy. But it didn't look like I could access it. "Why's it grayed out like that?"

"Remember what I said," Chak rumbled, sounding annoyed. "Everything has a price."

Frowning, I looked again and noticed words next to the icon.

Unlock this talent for 200 Blood Points.

I laughed. Figures.

Chak said, "Each class begins with one free talent. All other talents must be unlocked."

"I pay to unlock talents, then pay for levels so I can have talent points to put in them? Huh. Sounds like a racket."

"Racket?"

I shook my head and raised my hands. "So what you're trying to tell me is that I have to kill a lot of people to get the blood points to do all these things?"

"Correct," Chak said, grinning. Then he raised a finger. "I would advise you not to place your second talent point into Bash. Raise that ability later. Instead, save it."

"For when I unlock this Devil's Dance, then put it in there. Okay, now I gotcha. I'll wait." It annoyed me to act all chummy with this vile worm, but when in Rome...

Before I dismissed the talent-tree, I looked at the Passive tab which also had one grayed out talent.

Power Play 0/5

Cost: Nil

Cooldown: None

Increases Power regeneration by 15%.

Unlock this talent for 350 Blood Points

"What is Power?" I asked, dismissing the screen. I remembered I had 25 Power, already.

"Power is a type of stamina. You expend it when exerting yourself, like running or fighting. But also when you use some abilities, like your Bash. It is crucial to manage Power wisely. If you run out of in combat, you will be unable to fight or even defend yourself."

Again, I resisted the impulse to yawn in front of the maniac with the acid staff. All this information was a little overwhelming at the moment, considering I just murdered two men and nearly died.

Despite the info-dump, the fat slob hadn't shared anything that might get me out of here. I figured if I could progress through this story, or whatever this was, I might learn something. "So, you have another task for me?" Like finding the exit?

The pig shook his large head. "One more thing before we move on. Place your hand on the Life Crystal." He indicated the tall white crystal monolith which glowed on the other side of the pool.

Wanting to speed things along, I did.

Chasm Life Crystal

You are currently bound to this Life Crystal.

Upon death you will respawn at this location.

Note: When you die all unspent Blood Points, and all worn Marks, are lost.

My eyes widen at the last sentence. I lose everything? That's stressful. What if I wanted to save up for the next level or unlock a talent? I'd lose them?

I shook my head, not amused. Just when I thought this place was brutal enough, I find this out.

Chak grinned at my somber expression. "Yes, the price for failure is high. Very high, if you get too arrogant in your abilities. You suffer pain when you die, then suffer some more when you are brought back from the great beyond. Death is the way of the Realm, regardless of who you are."

This sim appeared to take great joy in making things most difficult for its players.

"So, I die and come back here," I said, having indulged that experience via tubby's acid staff. "Are there others? Seems like a tremendous pain in the butt to die in some faraway place, only to end up back here."

"There are many crystals spread across the Realm," Chak said. "You need only find one, and bind yourself to it. Then you will respawn at the new location. Although, you need to be careful here in the chasm, as I believe this is the only crystal available."

This time I sighed and made no effort to hide it. My mental faculties had been stretched to the limit since the ship was attacked and I'd been running full tilt since.

Chak scowled at my sigh. "Weakness is not becoming of a Berserker. Especially one under the Blood God! Perhaps you are not the right candidate for such an endevour." He flexed his grip on the staff.

Whoa, talk about a one-eighty. First minute he's a sagely teacher dispensing knowledge and the next he's borderline murderous.

I took a step back and raised my free hand, mindful to keep the club down. "Hey, easy there, big fella. I'm just a little tired, is all. My day has been eventful, to say the least."

"Tired?" Chak barked. "I'll show you tired you sniveling little-." He stopped, and suddenly turned his head to look up.

Keeping him in view, I glanced where he was looking.

Far in the distance the chasm wall stretched. Along its dark ridge, contrasted against the sky, was a sliver of bright red jewels. No, not jewels. Something else. As I stared, the jewels spilled down the wall, forming a red syrupy waterfall.

Lava.

It was too far away to be a threat, but it had Chak mortified.

"Damn," Chak said, his voice a mix of horror and revulsion. "He must know!"

"What?" I said, relieved I was no longer the focus of his anger. "Who must know what?"

"The Magma God," Chak said, lost in thought. "I don't know how, but he must." His blinked out of his trance and locked me with a determined gaze. "I suspect we are running out of time, Berserker. You'll have to learn as we move forward. If the Magma God is onto us, then we must move to phase two immediately. Follow me."

He turned and half-marched, half-waddled to the open gateway.

For the loss of anything else to do, I followed. "We're in phases?" I asked, catching up to him. "What was phase one?"

"Teaching you the way of the Realm and to prepare you for the coming conflict."

Okay. "What's phase two?"

He glanced at me as he hurried along the pathway, his eyes gleaming, but said nothing.

Fine, I thought. With little other choice, I followed.

CHAPTER SIX

As we hustled down the path to where, I had no clue, something bothered me. We were missing something. Then I realized it.

"Hey," I said, stopping. "There's something else you need to explain to me. I think it's important." Like where my ship is and how the heck do I get out of this nightmare?

Chak stopped, greatly annoyed. "What is it?" He cast a furtive glance at the distant lava flow cascading down the chasm wall.

I brought up my character screen and pointed at a line.

You have 2 unspent attribute points.

"I got those when I purchased the level," I said.

The fat man rolled his eyes in exasperation. "Yes, yes. Of course. I'd forgotten. And you are correct. They are important. Very important."

It made me feel a little happy to see this sack of dung admit he made a mistake.

He pointed at the screen which floated between us. "You must assign them to one of your four attributes. First is Might. Think of it as your strength. It determines how much you can carry, but more importantly, how hard you hit when attacking."

"So, I put them in Might?"

"Wait!" Chak barked, holding a hand up. His annoyance was growing. "Although Might is vital to close-quarters combat, Reflex is just as important. Reflex determines your speed and how fast you can move or dodge attacks."

He paused, expecting me to interrupt. I didn't.

Frowning, he continued. "Mind is mostly to do with magic and spells. It also is a measure of how smart you are. This is something your class does not rely on, but may become a factor in later levels. For now, ignore it."

The fact he told me to ignore it made it all the more interesting to me. But I kept silent.

"Finally, Vigor. This directly contributes to your overall health. More Vigor, more health points. It also determines how quickly you recover from sickness and ailments."

He stopped talking and looked over at the lava flow. I waited, counted to three, then I said, "So... where do I put these points?"

I expected him to snap at me, but he kept his composure. "Best to put one in Might, the other Vigor."

Nodding, I did as instructed. When I put the point into Might, nothing happened, nor did I feel any stronger. But when I did the same for Vigor, my health points jumped from 50 to 55.

"Oh, hey. Nice," I said.

Chak's scowled at my smile. "It just means someone can beat on you longer before you die." He waved his hand dismissively. "Enough of this, we must go."

Frowning, I followed after him. I wanted to prod him to explain the two skills listed on my character screen; Butchery and Hand-to-hand, but decided to wait. I didn't want to antagonize him into using that staff again.

We moved down the stone-walled path, approaching the turn.

"Wait a minute," I said, slowing. "That's where I fought those guys. That thing I saw could still be there."

The blood priest paused, as if uncertain. "Skaggs, no doubt. Not a problem if they are left alone." He pointed at the turn. "Go look."

No wanting to argue, I slinked up to the edge of the wall and slowly looked around the corner, just as I'd done earlier.

The clearing was empty. No bodies, no scary monster.

"Nothing," I said, and Chak quickly brushed past me.

We entered the clearing and stood at its center. The rocky ground was crisscrossed with bloody scratch marks and footprints. The woman's body left a complete impression in blood.

Chak looked over the macabre tableau, and smiled. "Beautiful," he whispered.

"What? This?" To me, it was anything but.

"It is like a work of art. A tribute to the Blood God. Your tribute!"

Oh, for crying out loud. Couldn't this guy dial it down a little? But with the word blood in his name, what else would I expect?

Instead of moving on, he felt compelled to say more. "Soon, you will make many tributes to the Blood God. Thousands! And he shall smile upon us-."

A noise from the other side of the clearing made us both turn.

From another gap in the stone wall, three men stepped into the clearing and spread out. They looked nearly identical to the two before. Burned men.

"Well, the Molten God glows brightly for us, my brothers," the tallest of them said. He gripped a club similar to mine in a large, charred hand. "A blood pig with his blood sow."

The other two chuckled and grinned. Neither were armed with anything I could see.

I turned to face them, planting my bare feet on the warm rocky ground, and hefting the bone club in my right hand. I felt more confident armed with it than the rock.

To my surprise, Chak didn't cower, or hide behind me as I expected. Instead, he looked at them with exaggerated disdain. "Look bitch, this fleck of burned skagg dung is speaking to us. How amusing."

Considering the situation, I let his name for me slide. But I resolved to have a long conversation with him about it later. If there was a later.

One of the other two burned men spoke up, both of whom were easily a head shorter than the first.

"The Molten God has been looking for you," Shorty #1 said with a sneer. "Figures you're the last priest. Wants you dead."

"Dead like your Blood God," said Shorty #2. "Ripped to bits, wasn't he? Eatin' alive?"

I felt Chak tense beside me.

The Tall One said, "Hey, that's right." He made a show of looking around the clearing, confused. "Where is he, your Blood God? Dead and dead. Ain't an easy thing killing a god. But yours was. Killed by the Molten God, may his heart always burn at the center of the world!" He raised his hands as he spoke, flakes of charred skin crackling off his body.

The other two did the same, chanting together. "May his heart always burn!" May his heart always burn!"

Are you kidding me? I thought. How much more goofy can this sim get?

I noticed Chak was getting angry and shaking. Suddenly he shouted at them.

"He was betrayed!" he said, spittle flying from his lips. "Betrayed by your god! They were allies! And like the craven the Molten God is, that simpering worm turned against him!"

I was amazed at how intensely he spoke, his rage boiling over.

The Tall One's grin widened. "Time for you two to join him. Dead god, dead priest, dead bitch."

I attacked.

Not out of bravery, but it was obvious where this conversation was headed. Being the first to the punch while everyone was yelling at each other made sense.

The distance between us was too short for me to have time to raise my club over my head, so I opted to use a tennis side-stroke. From waist height, I swung upward with all my strength at Shorty #2, the closest target.

Already itching for a fight, the trio weren't caught off guard, but my sudden attack made them hesitate for just a moment while their brains tried to play catch up with events. Unarmed, Shorty #2 couldn't counter and impulsively raised both his arms to try and block my swing. It kind of worked, too, deflecting the club away from his face, but not before I felt a satisfying snap.

Shorty #2 shrieked in pain as his left hand broke at the wrist, sagging at a painful angle.

As he turned away, the Tall One swung at me with his club. My forward momentum brought me within his reach, and the coarse top of the club raked down the left side of my chest and cracked off my left knee.

Sharp pain blossomed at the point of impact, but I still managed to twist out of the way of his backhand swing.

Shorty #1 roared and charged forward tackling me around the waist. Despite his size, he pushed me back several paces, slamming me hard against the stone wall. The air coughed out of my lungs and stars danced across my vision.

The little burned man kept me pinned against the wall, shouting, "Hit her! Hit her!"

The Tall One didn't need encouragement, and moved beside us to better angle his next swing. Unable to move or duck, it was all I could do to block him from hitting my face, using my left arm.

The club smashed directly in the crook of my arm, and I felt my elbow shatter.

I screamed in pain, my head thrashing back and forth. The movement saved my life as the Tall One swung at my face, only to glance painfully off my temple and strike the wall.

They're going to kill me. The thought rattled around my brain as if looking for a safe place to land.

Shorty #1, hands clenching my sides, took a step back as if preparing to slam into my again.

This brief moment gave me just enough freedom to swing my club at the Tall One.

I used Bash.

Without the ability, I might very well have missed. But regardless, my attack, coupled with Bash, caught the overly confident Tall One on the side of the head, right above his ear.

His skull caved in like a thick-shelled egg, and he instantly went limp, collapsing to the ground.

Shorty #2 saw this and changed from trying to slam me, to jumping on top of me. His arms wrapped around my shoulders, pinning my arms to the sides and causing me to drop the club. His legs locked around my waist and I stumbled back under the added weight.

I hit the wall again, although his limbs took most of the impact. Before I realized what was happening, he bit at the side of my head, latching onto my ear. Snarling, he bite savagely, wrenching his head back and forth.

Gasping in shock and pain, I screamed as he tore the ear off with a growl. My knees buckled.

But instead of sliding down the wall something in the back of my mind made me lean forward. It was enough.

We pitched over and slammed heavily onto the ground, Shorty #2 taking all of the brunt of it. He gasped, and I heard his head crack against the stone, but he didn't let go.

The fall slid him further up my body, and I found my face pressed hard against his shoulder.

Right by his neck.

Without thinking, I turned my head sideways, mouth wide. I bit into the side of his neck, scaly burnt skin scratching at my lips. The taught muscle was caught between my teeth and I heard him scream.

Now he released me, desperate to push me away.

But I wasn't done. Instead, I clenched to him hard with my knees and my still functioning arm, keeping him close.

Suddenly, thick arterial-blood gushed into my mouth and down my throat. My only reaction was to bite harder. I shook my head back and forth as he'd done with my ear.

Founts of blood geysered from the ragged wound and from around my lips as I made it bigger, exposing bone.

I felt the pounding of his rapidly beating heart which caused more hot streams of blood to shoot forth. Pulling back my clenched teeth, I tore away a wet hunk of flesh.

With a final gasp, he went limp beneath me, his arms and legs still twitching at his sides.

Sensing it was over, I pushed away from his body and over onto my back, coughing up blood and bits of burned man. What had I just done?

Suddenly, I realized there was still Shorty #1 to deal with. I pushed myself up to a sitting position and looked around, ready for another fight.

But the last burned man was gone. Only the Blood Priest remained, standing several paces away and looking like he hadn't moved a muscle throughout the entire fight.

"Where'd he go?"

Chak motioned at the entryway they'd come in. "Back through there."

I boggled at this statement. "And you let him *escape*?" Every inch of my body screamed with pain, and I couldn't feel my left arm or the side of my face anymore.

He shrugged, as if to say it wasn't his job. "I'm only a priest. You're the Berserker."

Incredulous, I barked a laugh, but only managed to launch into a coughing fit, hacking more blood up. Horrified, I spit and gagged as much out as I could. What if he had any diseases?

Chak knelt before me, his expression one of satisfaction. "You did well. Very well. You will make a good berserker. I shall heal you." He reached forward.

When I realized what he was reaching for, I batted his arm away with my good hand. He blinked at me in surprise.

I glared at him. "Not like that. Never again."

He stared, thinking. Then he nodded once. This time when he reached out, he placed his hand on my shoulder.

Chak has healed you for 5 Health Points.

Chak has healed you for 5 Health Points.

As he healed me, he said, "This little encounter has granted us an opportunity for you to learn something new."

"How to fight for my life?" I felt the weird sensation of my elbow clicking back together, becoming whole. An equally weird sensation on the side of my head made me check it with a hand. My ear was back, like it'd never been ripped off at all.

"No," Chak said. "Something very important." Finished, he stood back, giving me room to get to my feet.

"What? Fighting for my life isn't important?" I felt great. Like I'd never even suffered a scratch, let alone a near-death experience. His healing was almost like a drug.

Chak nodded. "Yes, but what's important is what you fight with. Not every fight grants you the chance to slay an opponent with just your teeth. Weapons are what you will really fight with."

"I thought I was the weapon?" I felt a little cocky after that fight. Three burned goofballs against one interstellar surveyor used to decades of a comfortable sleeping pods and gourmet coffee. How couldn't I be cocky?

He pointed at the two clubs on the ground, both partially submerged in puddles of blood. "Take those. We have to make this quick before we move on." He glanced around the clearing, as if searching.

I took the clubs, shaking each one off as best I could. They were coated in blood.

"Ah, there's one," Chak said and moved to a shallow recess between the stones. A bulbous glob of black rock spilled out from a fissure, former a large lump about waist high. Its top surface was perfectly flat.

Chak wiped a thick layer of dust away from the top, revealing gleaming facets.

I recognized what it was. "Obsidian?"

"Yes, obsidian, but more specifically, a crafting table. Place one of the clubs on it. Hurry now."

I put a club on the table-like surface, the bone clinking against the obsidian.

Suddenly, an information screen floated above it.

Simple Bone Club

Schematic Unknown

Learn Schematic for 50 Blood Points – Yes/No?

Introduced to yet more information to learn, I glanced at Chak.

The Blood Priest scowled. "Say yes, you stupid wench! What do you think we're standing here for?"

I flinched at the sudden outburst. Talk about a hot and cold personality.

"Yes," I said, resisting the urge to Bash the fat man right in the gut.

The club quickly dissolved into the table and vanished. Another message appeared.

Simple Bone Club Schematic learned.

Simple Bone Club:

3 units of Bone

100 Blood Points

Chak nodded, obviously satisfied. "Now you know the materials required to make this anytime in the future, although it is a dung weapon."

I stared at the requirements, concerned. "And where do I get these units of Bone?"

Chak pointed at the two corpses of the burned men sprawled on the ground.

I was afraid of that.

The Blood Priest squatted next to the short one, eyes scanning over every detail. Frowning, he snorted. "No. No good."

He went over to the tall one and did the same. This time his piggish eyes brightened. "Ah, here we are. Usable bone. Come closer, woman."

Not liking where this was going, but with little choice, I crouched down on the other side of the Tall One's body. His head was completely caved in at the side, his dead eyes staring up at the clouds.

"Now, look at him," Chak said.

"I am," I said, looking up and down his corpse. "He looks dead to me."

The scowl returned, but Chak made a visible effort to get his temper under control. Through clenched teeth, he said, "No, stupid girl. *Look* at him."

With a furtive glance at the staff in his hand, I did as asked, looking the body over, but more slowly.

Within seconds a glowing outline of the thigh bone appeared within the right leg. So did the lower bone of the left arm. It was like I stared directly through the body like a medical hologram.

"Huh," I said, I little surprised.

"Ah, you see the salvageable materials of their corpses," Chak said. "This is how you get what you need for all craftable items."

"But how do I actually get them out?" I asked, fearing the answer. Was I expected to hack the limbs of and tear out the bones? Could I even stomach that?

Chak laughed at my squeamishness. "Place both hands on the leg."

Laying the club at my side, I did as he said. I could see the glowing blue outline of the thigh bone floating within the flesh. The Burned Man's charred skin itched against my grip.

Another message, this one above my hands.

Salvage 2 units of Bone – Cost: 10 Blood Points – Yes/No?

"Yes," I said, uncertain what would happen next.

Amazingly, the man's entire leg simply vanished, leaving a ragged stump at his hip. In my hands was a heavy thigh-bone.

I didn't know whether to be impressed or to throw up.

"Good," Chak said. "Now do the same with the arm."

Keeping my thoughts to myself, I moved to the arm and repeated the process. The arm completely vanished, leaving a stump at the shoulder. I held the arm bone in my hands, and its information screen said it was 1 unit.

Chak stood, grunting with the effort. "Put them on the table and craft the club."

I carried both bones over and placed them on the obsidian's flat top.

Simple Bone Club
Requirements:
Units of Bone: 3/3
Craft this item for 100 Blood Points – Yes/No?

I said yes and the two bones dissolved into the obsidian. A moment later, a Simple Bone Club emerged where they'd been.

I picked it up. It was exactly the same as the one I'd been using.

Chak said, "This is how you will recover any lost items, whether dropped or lost after death. As long as you are willing to sacrifice the first item for its schematic, you can make it again and again as long as you have the materials."

I nodded. It was straight forward enough. I wondered what other things I would be able to make.

A hiss from somewhere nearby made Chak visibly blanch. "Hurry, they're coming. Best we move on from here."

I followed him out of the clearing through the entry way the trio had arrived from.

"Who's coming?" I said, apprehensive.

"Skaggs," Chak said. "Let us go. School time is over. Time to finally earn your place in the service of the Blood God."

I was about to ask what he meant when I heard hissing and the snapping of jaws behind me. Through the entry of the clearing, I caught a glimpse of something large and scaly.

What kind of a messed up place had I fallen into?

Knowing I wasn't going to get an answer right at that moment, and with a club in each hand, I hurried after the Blood Priest.

Could things get anymore bewildering?

Turns out, they would.

CHAPTER SEVEN

We followed the new path away from the clearing. Based on the high cliff walls on either side, it appeared we were moving down the length of the chasm. There were two new bright red lava falls in the distance, this time on the opposite wall.

Chak noticed them, too. "His influence grows stronger here. I should of suspected this would happen."

"Who?" I said.

"The Molten God, fool bitch!" he snapped.

For the briefest of moments, I nearly clubbed him over the head. "Don't call me that."

He glared at me, panting as he waddled along. "What? Bitch? Well, you are one. At least until you can prove your worth to the Blood God."

I kept my mouth shut. Not something I would do under normal circumstances. If anyone dared to refer to me in such a way I'd tear a strip out of them. In fact, I couldn't remember anyone ever calling me a bitch to my face. Besides, I wasn't one. Not even close. Interstellar surveyors were a patient, almost gentle, kind of ilk and I'd been one for years.

Of course, all that went out the window once I'd brained that burned man with the rock. But that was all a part of the circumstances I found myself in.

And what of the others? Caddie? Pullman? Were they still on the Corena? Could they also be trapped in this blood-soaked insanity?

And what of a rescue? It was a faint hope, and I knew it. We were far from the nearest system with a station. Even if the Corena had the means to send a Trans-light message drone back, it would take months to arrive. Then a rescue team would take months to get here. But what would happen to them? Would they be attacked by the planet, too?

Interstellar Surveying was the great Hail-Mary of occupations. You knew you'd be thrown far, far away from anything resembling human civilization without any real hope of aid should a crisis arise. And that's what I gladly signed up for. The pay was incredible. And the perks? Space travel, baby. Seeing brand new worlds and systems no human had laid eyes on. Relative independence. The higher-ups at corporate knew they couldn't micromanage crews who were light years away, so they gave us free reign to do as we saw fit. Within corporate guidelines, of course.

But they did have a means to keep tabs on their various crews aboard their incredibly expensive starships. Their Artificial Intelligences acted as defacto advisors on behalf of the corporations. The AI on each ship could never actually tell, or command a human crew what to do. That was against a myriad of AI laws which have been around for over a century. But they could suggest things and usually they got their way.

But what of Corena's AI? Otto? Was he still around?

Chak noticed me lost in thought. He snapped his fingers in my face. "Pay attention, foolish woman. Danger is everywhere."

I blinked in annoyance, but said nothing. I didn't want to get into an argument at that moment.

Chak glanced at the club in my left hand and stopped. "What are you doing with that?"

"Huh?" I said, genuinely confused. "I made this because you told me to."

"No, idiot. It's essentially useless to you right now. Drop it."

I furrowed my brow at him. "I went through a lot to make this damned thing. I'm going to keep it. Besides, two clubs are better than one, right?" I took a few practice swings with each, although the left did feel a little off. Was it the weight?

He rolled his eyes in frustration. "It is useless to you because you do not possess the Dual-Wield ability. Look at it."

I did.

Damage: 0 (Non-Dual-Wield penalty)

"What? It doesn't do any damage?" I said, annoyed. Was it broken?

"Until you gain Dual-Wield, any weapon used in your opposite hand will be completely useless. That's why I said to drop it."

"Isn't that a waste?" I said. "Why make it in the first place?"

"Bah!" Chak spat. He looked around, then spotted something. "There you are. Bring your cherished club over here."

I followed him over to a strange looking stone mound. It appeared as if it had been twisted into a form of a flower bud.

Chak waved a hand at the twist of stone. "Will it open."

"Huh?"

"Just think about the stone opening for you."

Okay. I did, and to my surprise, the folds of twisted rock actually unfurled outward, like an orifice. Within was a smooth shallow cavity.

"Put the club inside," Chak said.

With a shrug, I dropped the club into the cavity where it clanked loudly at the bottom.

"Close it," the priest said.

Without needing to be told, I willed the stone to shut. The twisted folds curled inward, grinding and popping. It sealed shut, looking as it did before.

"What was that all about?" I said.

"This is an inventory stone. You can find them everywhere. Placing items you don't need, or can't carry inside will keep them safe. And through the magic of the gods, if you find an inventory stone a hundred leagues from here, and open it, that club will be inside. As will anything else you put in."

Okay, that was a little impressive, I hated to admit. A global storage system. Kind of made sense considering I could only carry so much in two hands.

Not waiting to see if I had any questions, Chak marched off and I hurried after him.

Soon, the piles of stones funneling us along began to spread out, revealing narrow junctions and potential pathways. Chak ignored them all, his focus straight ahead.

I tried to see what was beyond the stone piles and caught glances of strange rock formations. Some were jagged, while others had long spikes that sprouted in every direction. They were all different shapes and sizes, but it was clear attempting to maneuver through them would be tricky. One misstep and you could be impaled or sliced open.

Not once did I see any vegetation, or anything like trees. In fact, since my arrival, I hadn't seen anything green. Just the dull grey of the rocks or the red of blood. It made me miss the sterile whites of the Corena's interior.

This sim needed a better color palette, I thought.

My eyes snagged on the little message list at the corner of my vision. I'd missed one during the fight with the trio.

You have learned a new skill: Clubs.

Advancement in this skill will grant bonus weapon damage with every 5% increment.

I looked under my skill list, and sure enough, it was there: *Clubs 1%*

I'd used my club for the first time during that fight which probably instigated the learning of the skill.

"Ah! We're here!" Chak said, eyes wide with excitement, yanking me out of my thoughts.

The stone piles ahead became more dispersed allowing me to see some kind of wide, flat hill beyond. It had an odd yellowish hue.

"Careful," Chak said, raising his hand for me to slow down. "We may not be the only ones here."

I didn't even know where here was, but I hefted my club and peered around as we walked forward.

We reached the edge of the strange hill which covered a large open area. Bizarre rock piles of deadly looking formations created a natural perimeter.

On closer inspection, it wasn't much of a hill at all, but a low mound, maybe twice my height. The yellowish material was of globular shape, like melted glass, forming cascading waves from the top.

Chak bent down and snapped a nodule of the substance that protruded out. He examined it closely, grinning happily.

"What is that stuff?" I said.

The Blood Priest suddenly licked the piece of yellow crap. "Ah!" he said, as if tasting something wonderfully sweet.

I asked him again and he said, "Excretion."

I felt my stomach lurch. "Excretion?" I looked at the huge pile of it. "What could excrete all this?"

Chak didn't answer. Instead, he stepped onto the material, testing it with his weight. "This is old. Very old. Come." He waddled up the mound.

Carefully, I placed a bare foot onto the stuff. It felt like hard plastic. I shrugged and followed him up.

Reaching the top gave a much better view of the surrounding area, but any territory beyond the perimeter formations were lost in the natural darkness the clouds above created.

The very top formed a round peak like the top of some mutated dessert. I was expecting to see a giant deep hole and was happy not to find one.

Chak looked the entire area over and grinned. "This is good. Now we can begin phase two."

"And that is?" I asked, not expecting him to answer.

"We dig!" he said, tapping his staff on the mound.

I looked down at the yellow crap beneath me. "Dig? Dig for what?"

Chak ignored my question. "First, you will need help. You doing it alone will take far too long, and your talents will be better served with other tasks."

I was not surprised he didn't include himself in the digging. "Tasks?" I was getting tired of always asking questions. Especially when he was selective on which he answered.

He turned to me and said, "I am going to give you a pair of quests. Each one will help us in completing this phase. After, we will-."

A shout cut him off.

We spun around to see two burned men appear through the perimeter and stop at the bottom of the mound. I recognized one of them as Shorty #1. He held his damaged wrist close to his chest and glared at me with pure hatred. With his undamaged hand, he pointed up at me and said something to his companion.

The other was bulkier than all the other burned men I'd encountered; his charred skin covering any definition of his muscular frame. In one hand he gripped what appeared to be an axe made of bone. It was larger than my club and likely more lethal. Down his left shoulder, and over his left pectoral, was a tattoo. Even against the ruin of his burned skin, it was prominent. A Mark?

"Ah, this is good," Chak said, nodding.

"Why is this good?" The large burned man looked far more dangerous than any of his other brethren.

"He is still injured," Chak said, indicating Shorty #1 and his shattered wrist. "That means they do not have a priest nearby to heal them. Once they're hurt, they stay hurt." He glanced at me. "I can't tell what Mark the other one has, so be careful."

I knew better than to ask if he was going to help.

Shorty #1 shouted at his friend, "Kill her! She's the one!"

The Big Guy suddenly bolted forward, climbing the mound.

Here we go. Not waiting for encouragement from the fat man, I moved downward to meet my eager opponent.

He growled as he ran up, but soon discovered the uneven material of the mound slowed his progress, causing him to stumble.

I carefully picked my way over the yellow crap, then realized how stupid I was being and stopped. Let him come to me; burn up all that energy doing so. Plus, I was above him. Didn't the warriors and knights of old favor the high ground?

Behind him, Shorty #1 followed, no doubt hoping to get a few hits in once I was down for the count. But I wasn't terribly worried about him; he wasn't the one armed with an axe.

As the Big Guy got closer, the mound got steeper. He huffed and puffed, his initiate burst of energy petering out. I waited, making a show of looking bored. Then, just as he got within arm's reach of me and swung his weapon, I quickly backed up.

The swing went wide, and he growled, storming after me. I continued to backpedal, allowing him to get within reach several more times. He swung when I did, and missed again when I simply stepped back.

But I couldn't keep this up forever. The mound was low, and we reached its pinnacle. Chak had backed away a fair distance down the other side, watching.

At the top, I stopped and prepared myself to fight. Big Guy, now covered in a thin sheen of sweat, growled and swung again. Despite my bravado, he managed to cut me across the chest. Blood oozed from the scratch; it hurt, but wasn't deep.

As he finished his swing, I countered with an overhand attack. But the very moment the club should have connected with his shoulder, he twisted his body out of the way, and I missed.

I was stunned. That should have hit him. I had dead to rights on him.

While I was momentarily surprised at his blinding speed, he suddenly altered tactics and swung a fist. I wasn't able to avoid it in time and he bashed me square on the nose.

Cartilage crunched and my head snapped back. For a second, I was dazed and stumbled backward. The movement saved me. He quickly followed the punch with a backhanded swing of the axe, and its blade swished through the air exactly where my neck had been a moment before.

I'd never experienced a broken nose before, and the pain was nearly blinding, but I couldn't do anything about it but fight on. Discarding all reason, and my own bodily safety, I lunged forward, club held high.

Big Guy's eyes widened at my sudden recovery, and raised his axe to block the blow. But I wasn't trying to hit him with the club. As he looked up, my knee connected hard with the hanging bits behind his loincloth.

I crashed into him as he doubled over. He staggered back, losing his footing on the incline. I shouted with glee, as he offered me the back of his neck for my club.

But as I was about to take him up on this generous offer, Shorty #1 appeared by my side. I barely registered the fact he was swinging something at me before it was too late.

He hit me right between the shoulder blades with a rock as I feebly attempted to twist away. But as I turned, I kept going, spinning three hundred and sixty degrees.

With both hands on the club, I brought it fully around at him. He had his hand up already for another attack, his face joyous at what he thought would be the final blow.

Just before my club hit, I used Bash.

I was rewarded with the sight of the weapon colliding fully with the side of his face. His head snapped to the side, and blood and teeth flew from his mouth.

As he tumbled away, I turned back to the Big Guy, who'd recovered enough from the knee to the groin to focus on me again, and who was already swinging.

His axe sliced through my left shoulder, through the muscle, and glanced off bone.

I screamed in pain, my eyes watering from the broken nose, and obscuring my vision. My instinct was to drop my weapon and grab at my gaping wound. Instead, I swung my club and, without thinking, tried to use Bash.

That ability is currently unavailable.

Big Guy was still close enough for me to connect with the swing, but, again, right when I should have got him, he somehow twisted his body enough to avoid it. The movement happened in the blink of an eye.

Why couldn't I hit this guy?

A tingle of fear blossomed deep in my chest as I made a cold realization: I was going to lose the fight.

As if to emphasis the point, Big Guy brought his axe down at my head, its blade covered in blood. My blood.

I don't know how, but I barely got my club up in time to block the strike. Our weapons struck with teeth jarring power. But the impact, causing us both to lose our grip. Club and axe suddenly bounced away to land on the ground.

Big Guy was stunned to suddenly be unarmed.

I wasn't.

Shrieking with blood-lust, I jumped up and onto him, just as I'd done to the burned man, earlier. I feared he'd do his magical twist again, and I'd miss.

But luck was on my side. I slammed into him and he pitched backward, losing footing. Wrapping my legs under his armpits and back, I latched onto his bald, burnt head with my hands. I wanted a jugular, but wasn't close enough, so I settled for what was available. With a growl, I bite hard into the bridge of his nose.

I am the weapon.

He screamed, and tried to pull me off, but lost his grip when we slammed onto the ground with him underneath.

I bit and tore and wrenched at his face. He desperately took a hold of my neck with both hands and started to strangle me.

I felt something pop beneath my jaw and I pulled, ripping away his nose and a large part of his cheek. Screaming, he released me and grabbed at the bloody ruin of his face with shaking hands.

Crazed, I spit his ragged nose down at him, then grabbed his head with both hands. As he flailed, I pressed my thumbs into his eyes.

He bucked beneath me, his death shrieks deafening.

I don't know how long I sat over him, both thumbs in his eye sockets as deep as they would go, bashing his head against the ground. But at some point, I noticed he was dead.

I slide off of him, my body slick with blood; both mine and his.

Coughing and spitting, I saw the horrific damage I'd done, but felt nothing but satisfaction. I'd won.

I blinked at this thought. What was happening to me?

Chak appeared, looking us both over, a wry grin on his face.

I knew what he was going to say even before he opened his mealy mouth.

"Good bitch," he said.

CHAPTER EIGHT

I sat in a daze as Chak healed me. Again, I'd been reduced to a blood thirsty maniac and indulged in such grotesque savagery it boggled my mind.

Yet, it didn't bother me as much as it should have. Perhaps I was simply accepting the vile requirements needed to survive. Still, I'd done things in the last few hours I would have never imagined in my most wildest dreams.

Or nightmares.

"You are a good weapon," Chak said, pulling me from my dour thoughts. He'd been quietly watching me. "The Blood God will be proud when I tell him of your efforts here."

"Oh, he will, huh?" I said, standing when the priest finished. I was whole again like nothing happened. "While you're at it why don't you mention how I want nothing to do with any of this crap. I shouldn't even be here."

"You have been picked to be here. You are a candidate selected by the Blood God."

I seem to recall it being the other way around. I had hurriedly selected my class and the Blood God before my arrival, not knowing what I was doing. Now I realized I should have been paying attention.

"You are aware I am here against me will, right?" I said, leveling the fat man with a glare.

He snorted. "Your will is meaningless. My will is meaningless. Only the Blood God's will is of any importance." Turning, he pointed at the two dead burned men with his staff. "These must be disposed off. They will draw skaggs here. But first, this one has a Mark you can claim."

Fine, change the subject, I thought. But I resolved to revisit the matter. I looked down at the Big Guy's corpse, and the bloody ruin of his face. By the stars, what had I done?

"You will need a blade," Chak said. "Take his axe and cut the Mark from his body."

I blinked at the directions. "Can't I just put my hands on it, like with the bones?"

"No, skin and hide cannot be salvaged. Only removed by skinning," he said, glancing around nervously. "Now hurry!"

I sighed, but didn't argue. Yet another indignity to blight my soul.

You have taken an item: Simple Bone Axe

Durability: Usable

Damage: 2-7

Tradable

Getting on my knees next to Big Guy, I looked at the tattoo. Its strange swirly markings appeared to be tribal in origin. I held the axe over the Mark, and hesitated.

Chak grew more impatient. "Cut! Cut, woman! It must be one whole piece!"

So I did. Cutting the skin off a human being was a lot easier than you'd think, if such horrific activities ever crossed your warped mind. In a few minutes, I'd cut an outline around the entire Mark, even turning the corpse on its side to get to it all.

Finished, I asked, "Now what?"

"Pull it free, but be careful you do not tear it or it will be useless."

The slab of skin came loose, but not without pulling tendrils of red flesh along with it. It was as if the body didn't want to give it up.

Satisfied, Chak said, "Good. There is some obsidian over there at the edge. Bring it with you."

I had the presence of mind to tuck my club under my arm, then, with the axe in one hand and a jiggling, bloody red flap of skin in the other, I followed him.

We stood next to the slab of obsidian and I noticed the twist of an inventory stone close by.

"Place the Mark onto the slab. Let's see what we have."

I dropped the sheet of skin onto the table with a splat, sending blood all over. Neither of us minded.

A screen appeared.

Mark of Dodge

+40% chance to Dodge skill

Claim Mark for 200 Blood Points – Yes/No?

I double checked my Blood Points. 480. I'd gotten 350 for Shorty and the Big Guy, the remainder from before.

"Claim it?" I asked, just to be certain. At Chak's curt nod, I selected yes.

The flap of skin suddenly dissolved into the obsidian and I immediately felt a light burning sensation on my left side. Twisting my head around to look, I saw the tattoo slowly appear on my shoulder. It was as if I was watching it being drawn on my flesh, one stroke at a time. In seconds, the full Mark was complete, covering my shoulder and chest down past my breast.

You have claimed the Mark of Dodge.

+40% chance to Dodge skill

Then another message appeared.

You have learned a new skill: Dodge.

This skill allows you to evade or avoid physical attacks. Additionally, an attribute bonus of +1 to Reflex will be applied for every 5% increment.

I marveled at my new tattoo. It looked... cool. Curious, I looked at my skill list.

Dodge: 41% (+8 Reflex)

My character screen also showed my Reflex was now 18, up from 10.

"Nice," I heard myself say. For a moment, I'd forgotten how I'd earned the thing.

Chak snapped his fingers at my face, causing me to flinch. "Pay attention, woman. There is an important fact you must remember. Marks are temporary. When you die, your body is taken by the gods and sent to the Life Crystal you are bound to. The price for your resurrection is all your Blood Points and any Marks on your flesh. So don't get used to them."

"Sounds like you expect me to die a lot," I said, admiring my tattoo. "Don't have a lot of confidence in your new weapon?"

"Don't be stupid. Death is a constant in this Realm. It drives it. It feeds it. It makes each of its denizens thankful."

"Thankful?" I said, arching a brow, prodding him. "Thankful for what?"

"Thankful for the gods to grant us purpose in our simple existence, by following their will until the final death."

I blinked at the flawed logic. "How can anyone be scared of death if they're just brought back? Resurrected? Other than avoiding the potential pain of dying, why worry if you simply respawn?"

Chak's expression melted into a scowl. "We are not all granted the ability of resurrection. Only those chosen by the gods have that gift."

Interesting. How did you know who would be brought back? And even more interesting, was Chak one of them?

But before I could quiz him further, he cracked his staff on the ground in irritation. "Enough of this blather. You have tasks to do." He pointed at the two bodies on the mound. "Remove them quickly."

"Remove to where?" I'd never had to think about where to dispose of a body before.

"Carry them out back onto the path we came from, and drop them out of sight. It should keep the skaggs at a distance."

"Okay, boss," I said. As I turned away I realized I still carried both the club and axe. The axe did more damage, so I put the club into the inventory stone alongside the other.

I hurried to the bodies and was forced to ponder the choice of dragging or carrying. Dragging would only tear them up along the ground, so I decided to carry one, selecting the Big Guy first.

Amazingly, I easily hefty his bloody corpse up and over my shoulders. I took a few tentative steps forward and found the weight easy to handle. Moving fast, I marched down the side of the mound and out into the path, all the while marveling at my strength. I'd never have been able to carry so much before.

Then it hit me. It wasn't my strength being used, but my avatar's, which was a lot stronger than I was in real life.

Shaking my head at the strangeness of the situation, I walked a short distance away from the mound and dump the Big Guy unceremoniously to the ground. A part of me felt horribly guilty for what I'd done to him, but that was quickly countered with the knowledge that none of this was real to begin with.

Back at the mound, I hoisted Shorty #1 up, finding him even lighter.

Chak was at the base of the mound on the opposite side, examining a strange looking pedestal covered in the yellow excretion. Seeing me, he fluttered a hand at me in annoyance, wanting me to hurry.

He can't be resurrected, I thought, as I marched down the hill, occasionally jumping with ease. He was like these burned men. A character that can be salvaged or taken by skaggs. Not a participant, or player. Like me.

Interesting, I thought, hurrying along the path.

Lost in thought, I turned the corner only to be confronted by a monster.

Large, grey and reptilian, the creature loomed over the corpse of the Big Guy. At first glance it resembled a monitor lizard, only immense in size. Its huge maw was open and a long red tongue extended from it to wrap around the bottom of Big Guy's legs. It had a pair of globular eyes which moved independent of each other. One watched the body it was pulling toward its mouth, the other fixed on me.

Did I mention it was huge? Easily four or five times the length of the Big Guy, from the tip of its wide blunt snout to the end of its thick whip-like tail.

My sudden appearance didn't even make it react other than to look at me with an eye.

Shocked, I watched transfixed as it easily pulled the Big Guy into its mouth. The body slid completely inside and vanished. The form of the corpse could be seen moving along its white, scaled, gullet.

An info screen appeared above it.

Carrion Skagg

Health: 100%

Magic: nil

Armor: 12

It had an armor stat, something I didn't. Looking over its scaly hide I could see very well why. It was like a segmented tank on four legs.

Finished with its meal, the skagg angled its other eye to me.

Uh oh. Even though it was about a dozen paces away, I didn't doubt it could close that distance fast. I took a careful step backward.

Its ropy tongue flicked out, then flopped to the ground, slithering in my direction.

You couldn't blame me for thinking I was its next intended meal.

I heaved Shorty #2's body off my shoulders and it landed a few feet away. The skagg's eyes fixated on the body, its tongue exploring it.

Not wanting to stick around to find out if it had any qualms about eating live prey, I moved back then ran. So much for salvaging the corpses for materials.

I reentered the clearing, my heart pounding. Wow. So that was a skagg. It was the reason the first set of bodies had vanished from the clearing; they'd been slurped up by a mutant crocodile.

Still a little stunned by what I'd seen, I wandered over to Chak, who was absorbed in looking over the pedestal. "Bodies are gone. Skagg ate 'em."

"Hmm," he said, lost in his inspection. The top of the pedestal was studded with several red rocks, like dull gems.

"I saw it," I said, when he didn't say more. "The skagg. It was gigantic!"

"They need to be in order to gulp down bodies," he said. "They always appear when a body is around. Always. That is why its best to salvage a corpse right after a kill before a skagg gets to it."

The priest ran his hand over the gems, caressing them and mumbling under his breath. Suddenly, one of the gems brightened like a light.

"Ah! Yes! Perfect. It slumbers, but can be wakened."

"What slumbers?" My eyes were drawn to the large yellow mound. "Whatever made that?"

Chak turned to me, annoyed. "Nevermind that. You will learn soon enough. Tasks. You have tasks to perform. So far, you have served the Blood God well, but his enemies are legion and are in need of purging. If you see any burned men or their ilk, slay them with impunity."

You have been given a quest: Slaughter the Enemy
Slay ten Burned Men and help weaken the power of the Molten God.
0/10 Burned Men Slain
Reward: 2 Skill Points

I would have thought that went without saying. Of course I'd kill them on sight. It's what I'd been doing so far, after all. It would have been nice if the slain counter on the quest was retroactive.

Chak waved a hand toward the mound. "This needs to be cleared and will require many hands."

"You want me to dig through all that?" I said, shuddering at the thought.

"No, that is not a task for you, but for slaves. Find and capture slaves, then bring them here. There should be some about, the burned men have many uses for them."

I remembered the two burned men eating the dead slave woman. Many uses was right.

You have been given a quest: Slaving Away

Round up a dozen slaves and bring them to the clearing to help dig. If there are tools present, bring them as well.

0/12 Slaves captured.

Reward: 400 Blood Points

"Where am I going to find them?" I said, looking around the perimeter. There were countless pathways that could be taken. But to where?

Chak scowled, annoyed. "Bah! Must I think of everything for you? Those two burned men came from somewhere, maybe a place with slaves. Head in the direction they came from. Now leave me be until you are finished!" He turned back to the pedestal, again, mumbling angrily.

Guess I'm dismissed. I left him there and tried to locate which pathway Shorty and Big Guy had come from. As I circumvented the mound, I gave it a sidelong look. What the heck could be inside that thing and why was Chak so interested in it?

Passing the crafting table and inventory stone, I paused, hefting the axe in my hand. Should I break it down for its schematic? It was better than the club in terms of damage and I liked the feel of its weight. Doing so would mean having to use the club, but I wanted to try out my new toy.

I shook my head and moved on to the path entrance, stepping through the rocky perimeter. Cautiously, I followed the new pathway which became very wide, all the while watching out for skaggs and burned men.

That skagg fascinated me. I'd never seen an animal so huge. And it was part of an ecosystem I'd only gotten a peek at. Still, I hoped to never run into one again.

As I walked around a high jumble of rocks in the middle of the path, I spotted something ahead. I froze, axe at the ready.

A burned man sat on a snarl of rock, his back turned to me. Next to him, growing on a mound of dirt, was a cluster of large green mushrooms. As I watched, he reached over, pulled one out by its roots and bit into it.

He hadn't noticed me, and I was initially uncertain what to do. I noticed the long thin spear propped up next to him, and the strange shirt he wore.

I squinted. Not a shirt. It appeared thick and was strapped to his body in a makeshift fashion with cord, or string.

Well, I am here to kill burned men. May as well add this one to the counter.

As quietly as I could, I padded over to him, practically tip-toeing my way. He didn't turn, so absorbed in his meal. Belching loudly, he reached over to grab another, then saw me from the corner of his eye.

Damn. He wasn't far away so I broke into a run, axe held high.

To his credit, the burned man only froze in surprise for a split second, then he quickly stood, dropping the mushroom. In an instant, he had the spear in his hands.

Unfortunately, I'd underestimated my speed and nearly ran into the spear as he thrust it forward. He should of had me, spearing me right through my guts. But at the last possible millisecond, as I attempted to get out of the way, I felt the Mark on my shoulder tingle.

My torso then twisted at an unnatural angle, something I shouldn't physically be able to do without snapping my spine. But I did, only catching the edge of the spear across my midriff.

Barely registering the pain, I brought my axe around and struck him in the back. He grunted with the impact, but his shirt seemed to take most of the blow.

Spinning to face me, he whirled the spear around in a wide arc, catching me off guard.

Again, he should have had me, or at least a piece of me. The Mark tingled again, and I quickly ducked, contorting my body as the spear passed over me head.

A clump of black hair landed on the ground. He'd sliced my ponytail off!

Not one to doddle in the middle of a fight, I sprung up from my crouch, axe traveling in an upward swing and used Bash.

The axe caught him fully under the chin. The bony blade easily crunched up through the jawbone to bury deep into his head from below. He went limp instantly, and fell to the ground, pulling the axe from my grip. Its handle stuck out of his face.

1/10 Burned Men Slain

I paused, breathing heavily. It all had happened so fast. The entire encounter had lasted five or six seconds, tops.

I stood over him, grimacing at his horrendous injury. I'd nearly sliced his head in half. Nasty. If it wasn't for the Mark of Dodge, I'd be fighting my way out of the blood pool right at that moment. Now I can see why the Big Guy so easily avoided my attacks.

I grabbed the axe handle, braced my foot against his chest, and pulled. It took several tries, but the axe came loose with a sickening sound. I frowned at the gore dripping from its blade.

I picked up the spear and tested its weight.

You have taken an item: Simple Short Bone Spear
Durability: Usable
Damage: 2-6
Tradable

It was strong and light, but would be almost ineffective once an enemy got in close, as demonstrated. I hefted it over my shoulder. It could be thrown, too. Maybe as an initial attack before running in with the axe?

I looked over the man's odd shirt. It was simply two large rectangular sections of what appeared to be hide, tide around his chest and waist with cord. No, not cord. Sinew.

Curious, I figured out how to untie it and pulled it off of him.

You have taken an item: Simple Ghourda Hide Shirt

Type: Light

Durability: Good

Armor: 2

Tradable

Armor! Finally. I'd wondered if such a thing existed, or whether everyone and their murderous uncle just ran around naked.

I ran a hand over the hide's surface, which was covered in very course hair. What was a Ghourda?

You have found a quest: Ghourda Skinning

Find and slay a Ghourda. Remove two units of Ghourda Hide and one unit of Sinew from its body.

0/2 units of Ghourda Hide

0/1 unit of Sinew

Reward: Simple Ghourda Hide Shirt Schematic

Well, now I'd know how to craft one, not that it looked difficult to make with the right parts.

I slipped the two sections of hide over my head and pulled them down over my body. Then I tied the sinew cords together as I'd originally found them. It was snug against the body, but the cut of the hide didn't hinder or limit my body's movement.

Armor: 2

Oh, that's new. I checked my character stats and sure enough the armor rating was listed there. I assumed the higher the number the better. The skagg had 12, a number which now had more significance to me. What if I could get a skagg shirt?

A message also appeared.

You have learned a new skill: Light Armor

This passive skill grants the wearer of any Light Armor a +1 Armor bonus with every 5% increase.

All that was left was the green mushrooms which got the burned man killed in the first place. They were large, like a muffin, and oily. I risked picking one.

You have taken an item: Green Mushroom

Consumable

Eating this mushroom regenerates 5 Power points over 30 seconds.

Tradable

I looked at my Power which was at 17. Running, fighting and using Bash had drained it. I'd no clue how long it would take to regenerate on my own.

Staring at the mushroom in my hand, I shrugged and took a tentative bite. It tasted like what I'd imagine plaster might taste like. Still, I finished it all and watched as my Power nearly topped up.

I also noticed that the wound on my side was closing up and healing on its own. The initial cut took 5 Health Points, of which I'd already regenerated 1.

My eyes snagged on all the messages I'd been ignoring at the corner of my vision and I glanced through them.

Since the last time I'd checked, my Club skill had increased to 3% and Hand-to-hand to 6%. Also, I'd gained the Axe skill which I apparently learned the moment I attacked the spear guy.

Spotting an inventory stone nestled behind a flourish of rocky spikes, I picked the remaining mushrooms and placed them inside. The spear wouldn't fit no matter how I tried to angle it. Guess I'd take it with me for now.

I checked over the corpse, but it didn't have anything to salvage. I'd leave it for the skaggs.

Carrying the spear and axe, and outfitted with new skills and armor, I moved on. All in all, it was a good haul for such a brief fight. I hoped the rest would be just as easy.

Only a few minutes later, I was brought up short by someone shouting at me.

"Can you hear me?"

I spun about, searching the area for who it was. The strangely distorted voice came from everywhere and nowhere.

"Who's that?" I shouted, tensing for a fight.

The voice spoke again, more clearly, and this time I recognized it.

"Captain! It's me! Thank the stars I've found you!" Otto said.

CHAPTER NINE

"Otto!?" I shouted in disbelief.

"Yes, Captain, it's me," Otto said. "I am so glad to have located you."

For a few stunned moments, I was at a complete loss for words. I wasn't alone anymore. Maybe now I could finally get some answers.

"Are you still hearing me, Captain?" Otto said when I didn't respond immediately. I was getting a little choked up.

"Yes! Yes, loud and clear," I said, trembling a little. "Give me a sitrep. What happened?"

"The planet somehow warped us directly to a low orbit around its equator. An incredible display of power. But, whether intentional or not, the Corena's hull began to immediately fracture under the sudden strain. I was in the process of initiating emergency protocols when the ship completely vanished."

My eyes grew wide as he spoke. "Wait? Vanished. The Corena is gone?"

"Correct."

"Then where are you?"

"Currently, I am orbiting the planet in satellite number six. A subroutine of the emergency protocols called for me to copy myself over to any other corporate entities in the immediate area, to maintain my files. Unfortunately, the satellite's hardware is tiny compared to the Corena's, and barely one percent of my program was ported."

I felt a chill shiver up my spine. "Okay, if the ship is gone, and your on one of the satellites, where the hell am I?"

"That is a tricky question, Captain."

"Humor me." The chill moved into my chest.

"Currently, you are standing within a chasm roughly two hundred kilometers north of the equator. The chasm happens to be the only feature on the entire planet. The rest is as barren, or blank, as before."

My breathing stopped. "Wait. I'm physically in this chasm. You can see me?"

"Correct, Captain."

"How can you see me on the planet's surface if I'm in a sim? Because that's what I've been experiencing for the last few hours; playing some star-blighted game!"

"Yes, I can see you, although it is only your biosignature. The strange cloud cover greatly distorts the satellite's sensors. But I'm at a loss as to what you are referring to as a sim."

I quickly gave him a bullet point version of what happened up until he contacted me.

"I see," Otto said, sounding concerned. "So you believe you've been logged into a sim, or game this entire time?"

"Yeah!" I said, alarmed and confused. "Are you trying to tell me all of this has been real?"

"That's the tricky part, Captain. Yes, you are in a chasm, and yes you are standing within it. But none of it is real. And neither are you. The signature is nearly perfect, but not quite. You are somehow controlling a copy of your body."

I found my head starting to hurt, and I slumped down on a large boulder. What the hell was he telling me?

When I didn't say anything, he said, "From what you just explained, I believe you really are in a sim, but unlike any seen before. It appears to be using a technology vastly superior to what is currently available. It is rendering the game world on the planet's surface. And rendering you as well."

Okay, keep it together Zee, I thought to myself. "So this is an avatar, right? This body?"

"Yes, but it is a physical rendition of it. By analyzing the electrical activity in your brain, I can see that your body is receiving messages, sent from a place I haven't located. I believe that copy is being controlled by you from an unknown location."

"So you are communicating to me through this body, correct?" I asked, thinking what a bizarre conversation to have.

"Correct. Perhaps your real body is still on the Corena, wherever it may be."

My mind boggled at this screwed up jumble of information. So all of this was real, yet simulated. Was that why I could feel pain?

Before I could ask another question, Otto suddenly said, "Captain. I am moving out of range. I can only manipulate the orbit of the satellite to a certain degree. On the next pass, I will attempt to make contact with you again if the cloud cover allows."

"Otto, what about the crew? Have you located any of them?" I found myself shouting to the air.

Silence. I called for him several more times, but nothing. I envisioned the tiny satellite scudding over head and disappearing behind the horizon.

What a lot to take in. Yet it was a relief to get some answers, even if they still raised their own set of questions. I already knew this was a game, but something far beyond mankind's capabilities. So, if humanity couldn't create this, who did? And why was I stuck inside it?

Lost in my thoughts, I didn't immediately notice the two burned men appear from around a cluster of rocks to my right.

One of them said, "Making enough noise, aren't ya?" His nose was a bulbous mutation that threatened to consume his face.

"If you wanna scream, we'll give you a reason," said the other. He grinned, revealing no upper teeth.

Both were armed with axes.

Why couldn't this damned sim just leave me alone? I felt a sudden rage build up inside me and I turned to glare at them. "Now isn't a good time, fellas. Save yourselves from a humiliation and piss off," I said, tightening the grip on my weapons.

"Ha! Listen to this one," Nose said. "Got some fight in her. I like when they try and fight back. Gets me all excited."

"Yeah, fight right up until we're done with you. Then we cut ya up and eat ya!" Toothless said.

As they spoke, I slowly switched the spear to my right hand.

Nose cackled. "Bet you taste good, too, huh? But first will jam you up with added flavor." He gyrated his hips and leered at me.

"That's a good one!" Toothless bellowed, overcome with the highbrow humor. "We're gonna jam her up with our fla-."

I stabbed Toothless through the throat. Sitting there, waiting for a chance to strike, I'd casually angled the spear in his direction. When Toothless turned to congratulate his friend, I lunged forward with it.

The spear pierced a jugular and lanced out the back of his neck. Gargling in shock and spurting blood, he fell back, eyes wide.

But Nose was quick, having anticipated an attack. With a short swing, he managed to hit me on the left shoulder as I'd lunged forward.

As Toothless fell back, the spear got stuck, and was pulled from my hand.

You have learned a new skill: Spears

Ignoring the message, I switched my axe back to my right right then swung at Nose, but he easily dodged it. My anger was almost blinding. Whether it was because I now knew for certain there was no immediate escape from the sim, or because of these idiots' taunts, I flew into a rage.

Nose and I traded swings back and forth for several moments. Sometimes I cut him, sometimes he cut me. But it became quickly apparent neither of us was getting the upper hand. The entire time, my Mark only kicked in once, saving me from having my throat slashed.

Consciously, I circled around him so he had to turn and face me. Then, I worked on making him back up under a series of swings. With his focus entirely on me, he didn't notice the body of Toothless until he tripped over it.

With a shout, he fell back, stumbling to keep his footing.

As he did, he lowered his guard. I jumped forward bringing the axe down over my head and used Bash.

The axe cleaved through his right collar bone and down into his chest, shattering his rib cage. He collapsed, but still tried to strike at me.

I batted away the feeble swing, then brought the axe down again and smashed his lower face, severing the jaw.

As the light went out of his eyes, I said, "How'd that taste?"

Standing over their corpses, I found myself at a loss as to what to do next. Thanks to Otto, I had a better understanding of my situation. The problem was the situation hadn't changed.

I had only two options. Sit on a rock and wait for Otto to eventually figure out how to get me out, or continue with the sim's silly story path which may lead to an ending. The ending might log me out, or shut the sim down, or something else entirely. I had no clue.

I wasn't a wait and see kind of person, so the choice was obvious. I'd play along until more answers were revealed. That was the only way I could have a hope of saving my crew, my ship and myself.

Trying to keep all the unanswered questions from cluttering my brain, I salvaged the two corpses, which yielded four units of bone. I also took their axes and went searching for an inventory stone.

Otto had keyed in on my biosignature, something which was considered unique to an individual. The closer you examined the signature, the more definitive it became. Yet, this body was a living copy of my own. How exact was it? Was it identical all the way down to the molecular level? A chilling thought, if not fascinating at the same time.

Finding an inventory stone and block of obsidian, I decided to sacrifice one of the axes for its schematic at the cost of fifty Blood Points.

Simple Bone Axe

4 units of Bone
120 Blood Points

I stored the bones and second axe, and took out a green mushroom to eat. The fight had drained me, and my Power wasn't regenerating fast enough for my liking.

As I did my best to ignore the taste of the mushroom, I saw the wall of the chasm in the distance. Lava spilled over its edge from dozens of falls. I blinked in realization as to what it meant.

The chasm was filling with lava.

It must have been the Molten God's intent. Maybe to thwart whatever it was Chak was conspiring, or perhaps to get to me. I was the player, after all.

This also meant there was a more definitive timeline to what I was doing. At some point the chasm would be flooded, and I had be far away from it when that happened.

I moved on, searching for slaves and burned men. If anything, working on quests kept my mind occupied.

Over the next half hour I encountered three solo burned men. Each eager for a fight, and each dying as a result. Before each fight, I'd used my trick of striking out with the spear with my right hand, the switching to the axe. I gained three clubs and six more units of bone. The price was high for those items, as my armor and Mark barely kept be from being sliced to pieces. My health was down to 55% and regenerating at a near imperceptible rate. I also raised my newly acquired Spear skill to 3%.

All the while, I watched as the lava flows grew bigger, and my mind screamed for me to come up with answers to all the new questions.

After placing my latest trophies into an inventory stone, I realized I'd been neglecting something, and checked my stats. I was sitting on a hefty 980 Blood Points which gave me enough to do two things.

I purchased Level 2 for 750 Blood Points, putting one attribute point each into Might and Vigor. Although increasing Might didn't have any obvious benefits I could feel, Vigor brought my maximum health to 60.

Then I spent 200 Blood Points on unlocking Devil's Dance, and dropped one of my two talent points into it. The cost to use the ability was steep, 10 Power, but helping me avoid taking hits for 5 seconds was great. I'd learned first-hand that a lot of attacks could happen in such a short amount of time. Couple that with my Mark of Dodge, and the next group I encountered would be in for a surprise.

I still hung onto my last talent point, not quite ready to committed it to either Bash or Devil's Dance. I'd decide on what to do with it after assessing the next bunch of fights.

As I walked around a small hill studded with rocky spikes, I suddenly spotted several figures across a small open area ahead, and froze.

Three people stood side by side, as if waiting. I blinked in surprise as I looked them over. None were burned men.

The man in the middle was short and stout. He wore a brown long-sleeved shirt, the first I'd seen. Everyone was either nearly naked, or wearing bits of leather or skin. He also wore trousers which covered him to his ankles, emphasizing the leather sandals on his feet. Without a doubt, he was the most well dressed person I'd encountered simply by having clothes.

But it was his two companions who gave me pause.

Although humanoid in form, they were the furthest thing from. They appeared to be comprised of nothing but bone wedged together to form limbs and torso. Each arm had at least ten or more sets of bone within it, like corded wood. Their chests were filled with dozens of sets of ribs, all mashed together forming a solid mass. Their entire bodies were like that, bones within bones.

Perched atop a neck comprised of several spine columns, was a single human skull which looked comically small to the rest of the body.

As I'd stepped into the open area, their skulls turned to look in my direction with empty eye sockets. Each wielded a large weapon in giant hands-within-hands. One with a large double-bladed axe, the other a strange double-handed sword made of a dark material.

I took this bizarre sight in for a few seconds, then prudently turned to run.

"Wait! Please!" the little man shouted.

Hesitating, I looked back, ready to bolt at the first sign of movement.

The little man grinned widely. "I only wish to trade! You have nothing to fear, I promise." He noticed me glancing at the two bone behemoths. "Oh, don't worry about them. Their harmless. Just as long as you don't try to steal from me, kill me, or eat me, they'll give you no bother. Please. Come see my wares." He waved a beckoning hand.

Every fiber of my being told me to run away, but the man's oddly pleasant nature, and the fact neither guardian had made a threatening motion, made me reconsider.

I shouted, "Who are you?"

Seeing I wasn't about to run away at that moment, the man's grin got even bigger. "I am Jax, trader of goods and wares! And might I ask your name, great warrior?"

"Zyra," I said, still uncertain. Could you blame me?

"Ah!" Jax said. "A mighty name for a might slayer such as you. No doubt you are in need of wares to grant you a swift victory over your opponents. Come, see what I have." He turned to an open inventory stone behind him, and began to take items out of it, placing each one on a large mat on the ground.

Okay, I thought. This was all kinds of odd. Yet, unlike every other person I'd encountered, they didn't attack me on sight. I took it as a good sign.

Shrugging, I decided to check it out, but resolved to keep my guard up.

Warily, I approached, crossing the clearing. As I did, the skulls of the two giant beings tracked me and I could hear bone grinding against bone.

At ten paces away, I stopped and looked at one of them.

Bone Golem (Summoned)
Health: 100%
Magic: nil
Armor: 20

Wow. Their armor was insanely high thanks to all the densely packed bones. I couldn't imagine causing any damage to them before they cut me in half with their huge weapons.

"Who're your friends?" I asked, feeling tiny before them.

"My bodyguards," Jax said, as he placed the items. "It's dangerous business being a trader in the Realm. As someone who's career is based on trading items of value, I need protection from those who would relieve me of my hard earned wares. These two do an ample job of that."

"I don't doubt it," I said, eyes wide in awe. They were gigantic.

Finished, Jax said, "Here is what I have to offer. Not much, compared to some, but I'm sure each could be of use to you."

Curiosity got the better of me, and I took a few steps closer. I could see several items spaced out evenly on the mat. Suddenly, a list appeared before me.

Jax's Items For Trade:
1 Skull Cap
3 Blood Berries
5 Simple Bone Axes
9 Simple Bone Clubs
10 units of Sinew
45 units of Bone
2 units of Molten Glass
1 unit of Skagg Scale

Jax said, "What do you think?" He seemed quite proud of the selection.

"Uh," I said. "To be honest, I don't know what to think. I recognize some of them."

"Feel free to have a closer look."

With a glance at the Golems, I went to the edge of the mat and selected an item.

Skull Cap
Durability: Good
Armor: 4
Tradable

It lived up to its name; it was a skull, less the jaw bone, but exaggerated in size. A cord of sinew dangled from a hole drilled on one side.

"You wear this?" I said, a little baffled.

"Yes, let me show you," Jax said, unfazed by my stupid question. He took the cap and slid it over his head. His eyes looked through the large hollowed out eye-sockets, and the teeth of the upper jaw covered most of his mouth. He pulled the cord up beneath his chin and tied it to the other side, keeping the cap in place.

"See?" he said, his grin never fading. "This should keep you from getting your head split open or bashed in." He rapped his knuckles against it. "Only the most prudent of fighters go into battle with one."

Although it looked ghastly, it appeared to offer some protection to the head. Something I could most certainly use.

"How much?" I asked, clueless to how currency worked here.

"10 units of Bone. A steal, I must admit, but for someone as obviously intelligent as you knows a bargain when she sees one."

So items were traded for other items.

I picked up one of the berries, which resembled a dull red grape.

Blood Berry
Consumable

Eating this berry will heal 10 health points over 60 seconds
Tradable

Oh. Now this was something I definitely needed. "How much?"

"One unit of Bone each. Not only will these berries keep you alive, they are most delectable, too!"

Suddenly, a large hissing from behind the nearby rocks made us all look, the Golems' skulls swiveling completely around.

A dim red haze revealed huge lava flows in the distance.

"Damn!" Jax said. "Such a waste. Now I'll have to move on and find another place to set up business." Although he sounded annoyed, his grin never wavered. "Perhaps we should finish up while we still have time?"

I waved a hand at the Molten Glass which looked like small bulbous trinkets. "What are these?"

"Ah! Perhaps you haven't the pleasure of crafting an item which needs them. Very important for that and quite rare. Thirty units of Bone each."

I indicated the Skagg Scale which was deep grey in color and as big as my hand. "That is used in crafting, too?"

"Very much so. It is a highly sought after component for various armor schematics. Again, very rare. One hundred units of Bone."

All this need for Bones for trading. I didn't miss the underlying message. In order to trade for useful items or weapons, you needed a lot of it. And the only way to get it was to slay more enemies.

As I pondered what to get, Jax cast furtive glances at the distant lava flows.

"Okay, I'll take the Skull Cap and the three Blood Berries."

"Excellent choice! Wonderful!" he said, positively beaming. He looked me over. "Uh, is the Bone stored?" he said, waving at the open inventory stone.

When I said yes, he nodded and went over to close it. "There you go." I realized he'd just closed his own personal storage vault, allowing me to access mine.

We made the trade under the watchful gaze of the Bone Golems.

I ate one of the berries and nearly gagged. It tasted like blood. Another aptly named item. Despite feeling revolted, I finished it. Now my health was almost at one hundred percent.

Jax returned his items into the stone, then rolled up the mat and placed it inside, too. Clapping his hands clean he turned to smile at me. "It has been a pleasure doing business with you. This was a far better experience than dealing with those idiotic burned men."

"Really," I said. "What did they want?"

"Slaves," he said, matter-of-factly. "Mostly for mining of Molten Glass, but also for other things."

"You sold them slaves?"

"Traded. And at a high cost, too. But with the backing of their god, they could afford it."

"Where did they go, these burned men?"

He pointed toward the distant chasm wall. "That way. I suspect their trying to get as much of the glass as possible before the lava arrives. Which is my cue to leave," he said with a bow. "May our paths cross again, mighty slayer. I must go now to find other customers."

With that, he turned and walked across the clearing, one Golem leading the way, the other trailing behind, their skulls swiveling. I realized I should have asked if he had anything that would allow me to carry more items, but it was too late, and put the two Blood Berries into the stone.

As I slipped the Skull Cap over my head and tied it on, I looked in the direction he'd pointed.

Now I knew where to go.

Hefting my axe and spear, I ran off into the darkening haze.

CHAPTER TEN

It didn't take long for me to find them.

The relatively flat terrain helped me see movement through the rock piles in the distance. Squinting, I couldn't make out exactly who was ahead, but there were several of them.

Carefully, I picked my way forward, using cover to get close enough for a better look.

Over a dozen people were in a large flat area, barren of rocks. Seven were immediately identifiable as burned men by their horrific skin, and the weapons they carried.

The other six were human, but not burned in anyway. These people wore strange black cords strapped to their bodies, like harnesses. Each used a pick-like tool to dig into a low mound of dark glassy rock. I focused on one of them and managed to get an identifier.

Male Slave
Health: 74%
Magic: nil

As I watched, a burned man approached the slave and hit him in the back with the butt of a club, yelling at him to work faster. I noticed these slave drivers giving the approaching lava worried glances. It seemed they were on a timetable, as well.

From my hiding spot, I scanned over the scene. Six slaves and seven burned men. I'd never encountered a group this large and it worried me. Even if I could assume the slaves wouldn't join in any fighting, taking on seven armed combatants at the same time was intimidating. Three had been a painful challenge, despite winning. Seven would be a whole other level of pain. But I had a Mark, some armor, full health, and a new talent ability. But how to go about it?

Charging straight at them was potentially fatal as they'd easily swarm me. I could wait and see if any left the area out of view of the others and eliminate one or two that way. But the burned men looked to be too keyed in on the slaves to go for a casual walk among the rocks.

After more observation, I realized that the low mound could obscure my approach if I came in at a different angle. The slaves were spread out in a wide semi-circle along its base, hitting and picking at its glass. The burned men stood in a loose line behind them, with two or three occasionally pacing around the other side and out of view.

Okay, then. The tactical approach it was.

I slinked my way behind the rocks to a position that was close to the far end of the line of slaves. This put two burned men behind the mound, with a third looking in their direction, talking. If I did it right, I could charge forward and eliminate one or two before the others even realized what was happening.

I paused, taking deep breathes. My heart was already ratcheting up, the adrenaline pumping. Crouching low, I waited for the right moment, rocking back and forth on my feet.

When it looked like most of the men were looking away, I sprung from my hiding place and into the open.

Sprinting like a madwoman, I raced over the short distance.

My intended target was the burned man at the end, and I was coming at him from directly behind. Amazingly, none of the others noticed me.

As it turned out, it was a slave that gave me away.

A woman, toiling away listlessly at the glass, caught sight of me, and she froze. Her eyes widened as she stood, staring right at me.

The man I was charging at noticed and yelled at her to get back to work, then clued in to her odd behavior. To my right, I heard a shout, but ignored it. I was committed.

The man looked away from the slave woman and turned around.

That's when I slammed into him with the spear with the full momentum of my body. We collided, the spear in my right hand passing straight through him to stick out his back.

Unfortunately, I was going too fast, and we both fell to the ground, him underneath. I heard a loud crack – the spear had snapped.

When we hit the ground, I managed to roll forward over him and came to my feet. I spun about to see the next burned man gaping at me in total shock. Behind him, the others were rounding the mound.

I am the weapon.

Charging at him, I switched the axe to my right hand and raised it high. I heard someone screaming like a crazed banshee, and realized it was me.

The burned man was rooted to the ground, still stunned as I came within striking distance of him. But he snapped out of it, and raised his axe to try and block my swing.

I slashed him across the chest, then used my forward momentum to ram into him with my right shoulder. I heard several of his ribs crack with the impact and he fell backwards, gasping.

I couldn't follow up because another man was suddenly on me, swinging his axe and yelling. His first attempt cut deep into the hide shirt, but I didn't register any pain. The swing brought his head close to me and, unable to swing my axe in that moment, reached up with my free hand and jammed my thumb into his eye.

There was a soft squishing noise, and I felt my thumb hit the back of his eye-socket. He twisted away, shrieking in pain.

Again, I couldn't follow up, as the rest of the gang had arrived.

Grouped together the four others surged at me, causing me to backpedal fast. They swung their axes wildly, eager to get at me.

I was hit two or three times, and each came with a dull pain. Whether they drew blood or not, I didn't know, or cared. I was deep in the heat of the moment.

And loving it.

The taller of the four managed to aim a swing right at my head, and I half-ducked, half-blocked it. His axe cracked firmly down on the my forehead, and I felt the skull cap crack.

An explosion of stars blinded me, and I staggered, desperately swinging my axe in front me to keep them at bay.

That's when the Mark worked its wonders.

Even though I couldn't see it, someone slashed at me with a sideways swing. It should have eviscerated me, ending the fight right there. But as I blindly swung about, I felt the Mark tingle on my shoulder.

The next moment I found myself leaping upward and sideways, my body spinning like those ice skaters of old.

I felt the swing pass through the air directly beneath me.

The Mark may have helped me avoid the attack, but it didn't help with the landing.

I spun in the air, then fell hard to the ground. This should have been a death sentence.

They were on me in an instant, swinging and kicking at me. I caught a lot of the blows, but instinct took over and I thrashed about like a rabid tiger. For each swing that hit me, I gave two hits with my axe. This pushed them back a little which helped because I needed to get to me feet or I was dead.

As I staggered up to a standing position they surge forward as one.

Use Devil's Dance

I'm not sure how to accurately describe the next five seconds. The moment I used the ability it was like the Mark of Dodge, but with the power of a Trans-light drive.

I easily evaded each and every swing they put to me. My body spun and twisted away from attacks which should have landed. I danced like the devil, as it were. And as my body performed these insane magical contortions, evading blows, I attacked. Swinging my axe and connecting each time.

But the five seconds flitted by and I felt an axe glance across my lower back. No more magical evasion.

Still, two of the burned men were dead on the ground, blood spilling from fatal wounds. The other two were hurt, but still determined.

As one lunged to catch me as I slipped in a puddle of blood, I used Bash. Although I lost my balance, my axe powered through his attack and buried deep in his chest, cracking through the sternum to the heart. He fell to the ground, but my axe was still in him.

The last man swung at me and I danced back, desperately looking around for another weapon. I suddenly noticed he had a Mark across his stomach. What could it be?

As he came at me, I quickly snatched up another axe from the ground, but not without getting cut across the back of the left arm for my efforts.

I spun about, catching him across the chin with the very tip of the blade. He grunted, but kept coming. As we dodged and swung, I saw I'd really cut him up badly, but despite all that, he fought on.

For at least two minutes we fought. I hit him more than he hit me, yet, he stayed on his feet. To be honest, he'd taken more damage than any opponent so far.

But we were both slowing down, the adrenaline in our systems petering out. He and I were at the point of exhaustion.

Why wouldn't he just die already?

Finally, he took a wide, tired swing, giving me an opportunity. I ducked the swing and came up from beneath it. My axe slashed across his throat, and arterial blood exploded from the wound, drenching me.

He collapsed to the ground, spasming, holding one hand to his fatal wound in a feeble attempt to stanch the flow. In seconds, he was dead.

I fell to the ground, gasping for air and bleeding from a dozen wounds. A glance at my health told me what I already knew.

2%

I had only one chance. Before, while I was watching the burned men from my hiding spot, I saw an inventory stone near a small jumble of rocks. Groggily, I looked around for it, my vision blurring. When I found it, I crawled.

So focused on my destination and the fact I was at the point of death, I didn't even notice the slaves watching me from a distance. Once I reached the stone, I had to drop the axe in order to heave myself up over its lip to access its opening.

I gobbled down the two Blood Berries like they were food from the heavens.

As I sat there, slumped against the stone basking in their healing effects, I checked one of my stats.

Power: 1

Well, there you go. Thanks to using both my abilities, which sucked up Power, and fighting seven energetic opponents, I'd brought myself to complete exhaustion.

Fine, I thought. I had a fix for that. I ate some of the green mushrooms as quickly as I could. My stomach ached from all the food.

Finished, I pulled up my Passive tab, bought Power Play, and dropped my last talent point into it. It wouldn't be a major booster to my Power regeneration, but it was better than not having it at all.

Movement to my left caught my attention.

Shockingly, one of the burned men was still alive, and crawling across the ground toward me. His face was drenched in blood.

Then I remembered he who's eye I'd jammed my thumb into.

He looked very angry as he crawled across the uneven ground, cutting his legs and hands in the process. But he didn't care. He was after me.

"You bitch!" he spat.

With an exaggerated sigh, I pushed myself up to my feet. I waited a few moments as he crawled closer, then I made a point of slowly bending over to pick up the axe.

"The Magma God will consume you!" he said, still coming. "Your flesh will burn for an eternity!"

Zealots, I thought, slightly bemused. Bored of his ranting, I walked over and easily dispatched him with several quick blows.

I looked over the grizzly carnage. Seven dead bodies, weapons and puddles of blood mixing together. The Devil's Dance proved its worth, as well as the Mark.

The slaves hadn't fled as I expected, instead clustering together and staring at me like frightened children. I wasn't sure what to say, as this wasn't a rescue mission. They'd been slaves for the burned men and now they were mine.

Uncertain how to process that, I quickly picked up all the axes and placed them in the inventory stone. But as I started to look over the first body to salvage it, I heard a sobbing coming from the slaves.

Their terrified expressions pulled me toward them and I tried to calm them down.

"It's okay," I said, yet knowing different. Based on what Chak wanted to do with them, they'd simply go from digging one mound to another. When I looked any of them in the eyes, they quickly averted them, trembling. They were filthy, naked and strapped in their strange harnesses.

I moved closer, free hand raised. Although I sensed they wouldn't attack me, I kept the axe at my side.

The crying intensified, coming from a man crouched at the rear of the group, his back turned.

"Hey, it's okay, you're safe now." The others parted, flinching at my every move.

The man's body racked with sobs. I worried he wouldn't be able to move and I didn't feel like sticking around to babysit.

I touched him on the shoulder, and he spun around to look up at me.

I gasped.

Despite his face being streaked with tears and grimy dirt covering every inch of his skin, I instantly recognized him.

Pullman.

CHAPTER ELEVEN

He gaped at me, terrified until I realized the skull cap partially covered my face, so I removed it.

"C-captain?" Pullman said, eyes wide.

"Pullman!" I said, surprised. He was here in the sim with me. But what relief I felt in that moment evaporated when he suddenly burst into tears.

"Oh, Captain, I'm so glad you're here! It's been terrible!"

I blinked in confusion. I'd never seen the man cry before. Over several years of surveying together, he'd barely shown a hint of emotion. "It's okay, Pullman," I said, a little taken aback. What was wrong with him?

"I- I thought they were going to kill me," he said, wiping snot from his nose with the back of his hand. The motion was limited by his harness.

"Well, they're not going to now. They're dead," I said, and felt a pang of annoyance. He'd been standing here the whole time I fought and didn't help? That wasn't like him at all. He'd served twelve years in the Stellar Corp as a dropship marine. Seen combat dozens of times. An injury forced him into early retirement where he found his way into interstellar surveying. This was a man used to blood and death. But seeing him blubber like a baby gave me pause.

"Pullman, what happened to you?" Maybe if I let him tell his story, it would help.

He calmed down a bit, sniffling. "What happened to me? I got kidnapped is what happened. One minute, I was in engineering, tooling up the impulse engine as you asked, then this white light filled the section. Blinding. The next minute, I found myself here, in this spot, tied to these people. I was confused as all hell, no clue as to what was happening. Those bastards with the crispy skin immediately jumped on me, beating me almost senseless. Commanded me to dig at this stuff. I was completely shocked! I still *am* completely shocked!" He broke into tears again.

I watched him, confused, trying to sort out what he said. "So, did you select a character to play? A class?"

"What are you talking about? I didn't choose to have this happen to me!"

A faint spark of angry flickered at the back of my mind, but I pushed it down. The man was traumatized. I needed to go easy on him. "Pullman, this is a sim. We're playing a damned sim. You know that right?"

"Of course I do!" he suddenly snapped. "I'm not daft you know. Just a little overwhelmed by it all. I figured it was some kind of program or sim when I could pull up information screens on people and things. Not that any of it is useful. I can't find a way to log out!"

"Have you seen any of the others? Caddie or the rest?"

He shook his head, miserable. "No, no one. Just you." His eyes looked over at the bodies. "You really messed those boys up, Captain. I've never seen anything like it before. You moved like a tiger jacked up on stims."

For some reason, talking about my fighting ability made me feel uncomfortable. Probably because I was an Interstellar Surveyor, not a mass-murdering crazy woman. I changed the subject. "We're on the surface of the planet."

"What?" he said, baffled. "Not a sim on the ship?"

"No, the planet is part of the sim, or so we think. Otto is in a high orbit scanning its surface."

The exaggerated expression of relief on his face was almost comical. "Otto is here?"

I nodded, then gave him a very quick breakdown of everything that'd happened to me since the ship was attacked. He listened intently, mesmerized.

Once I'd finished, he nodded enthusiastically. "Okay, this is starting to make a lot more sense," he said.

"It does?" I said, surprised. "Because I'm still in the dark."

"No, I mean this place and why I'm here. I've been at a complete loss until you explained it." He looked thoughtful for a moment, then said, "You got to select a class and god, but I didn't. What does that mean?"

Good question. I had no clue. But something Chak said about my respawning tickled the back of my brain. "Pullman, have you been bound to a Life Crystal?"

"No, not as you explained it. I haven't."

I looked around at the slaves who hadn't moved an inch from their spots the entire time. "Does anyone know if there is a Life Crystal close by?"

Their terrified looks told me I wouldn't be getting any answer from them.

"They don't speak at all," Pullman said. "Their tongues are gone; cut out."

Damn. It made them look all the more piteous to me.

Pullman stood, wiping tears from his cheeks. He was no longer crying. "I thought they'd do the same to me, those men. But it amused them to make me say things for them, then threaten to cut me like the others. Why are you looking for a Life Crystal?"

"For you," I said, and looked off at the approaching lava flow in the distance. It was getting much closer. "I'm not sure what will happen to you if you die in this sim. I respawn because I'm bound, but I don't know about you."

"Well, let's not find out, then, eh?" he said, and for the first time, grinned.

A hissing noise made me spin about.

Skaggs. Four of the giant creatures were clamoring over rocks and entering the area. Their focus was on the bodies.

Both Pullman and the slaves gasped. I held my hand up for them to be quiet. "They're not here for us, they just want the corpses." I wanted those bodies, too, to salvage. But that wasn't going to happen now.

"What are they?" Pullman said, horrified. One of the skaggs roped a corpse with its tongue and deftly slid it into its massive mouth.

"A problem if we stay any longer," I said. "Everybody get to the other side over there!" I motioned to the area I'd first entered from.

Thankfully, the slaves moved without further encouragement. Pullman stayed along side me. The harnesses limited their movements and each still carried a pick axe.

"Where are we going?" Pullman asked.

"Away from here," I said, keeping myself between the skaggs and the slaves.

"Back to that Chak fellow? Doesn't he just want a bunch of slaves, too?"

I found myself not wanting to answer the question. Then I realized something. "Wait! Stop here." We were at the other side of the area, standing between tall pillars of stone.

"What? What's wrong?" Pullman said, alarmed that we weren't still running from the monsters.

I scanned over the bodies, slipping the skull cap back on. "I forgot something."

"Are you joking?" Pullman said.

I wish I was. Then I spotted the body of the man with the Mark on his stomach. He was right in the middle of the area, surrounded by skaggs. I couldn't explain why, but I had to get that Mark.

Disregarding any sense of logic, I said, "Stay put. I'll be right back." Then I ran toward the skaggs.

"Captain!" Pullman shouted, but I ignored him.

The four skaggs were busy dining on burned men. Each creature had a different set of colored scales; white, grey, black and green.

As I approached the body, the white skagg turned toward me. A burned man's head vanished over the lip of its mouth, the form of the body sliding down its gullet.

I slowed, trying not to look menacing. Its globular eyes swirled about, one on me, the other on the body between us.

This is mine, asshole, I thought. Carefully, I reached down and grabbed the body by the arm, gripping the wrist.

At that moment, the skagg opened its mouth and its long pink ropy tongue whipped out, wrapping around the body's legs by both ankles and squeezing them together.

I glanced down at the Mark. It was mine. I earned it. Then I pulled at the body, trying to drag it away.

The skagg seemed momentarily baffled by me, then took a step back, pulling with its tongue. The body between us lifted off the ground. For several moments, we had a tug of war with me trying to dig my feet into the hard ground.

The skagg was infinitely stronger, managing to get the legs of the body into its mouth up to the man's waist.

I still hung on, even dropping my axe to grab the other wrist. Around me, I heard hissing and the scraping of claws on stone. The other skaggs were still feeding, but their distraction wouldn't last.

Somewhere in the back of my mind, a small voice was asking what exactly did I think I was doing, but I ignored it. I wanted that Mark.

The skagg's initial bafflement didn't last. Annoyed, it snapped its jaws together, biting deeply into the body's waist. Giving further claim to its prize, it twisted its head and pulled.

It dragged me along with it, and shook my from side to side, but I still wouldn't give up.

Suddenly, I heard a wet tearing sound. The body ripped across its middle. With both of us pulling hard, it tore apart.

I flew back, falling to the ground, the torso landing on top of me. A ragged spinal column stuck out from below its navel, blood and innards spilling out. The skagg, momentarily mollified, slurped down its half of the body.

Not wanting to wait and see if it wanted more, I got to my feet, and sprinted away, slinging the torso by the arms over my shoulder.

As I approached the others, I could see the look of complete horror on their faces. "Let's go!" I shouted. "We need to get some distance from them."

Not wanting to disobey the maniac woman carrying a bloody torso around, they ran, Pullman included. I glanced back. The skaggs had devoured all the bodies and were snapping at one another. The white one didn't pursue me, but I didn't want to take any chances. I followed the others.

A short distance away, we came upon an inventory stone and slab of obsidian. I called for them to stop, then dumped the torso on the ground. To my amazement, the Mark hadn't been damaged.

Pullman stood beside me, eyes wide. "Captain, what have you done?"

I pulled a replacement axe out of the stone, then crouched beside the torso. "It's not what I've done, but what I'm going to do." Carefully, I sliced around the edges of the Mark.

Pullman swayed on his feet, then lurched away to vomit behind a rock.

Cutting the last of the Mark free of the skin, I marveled at how quickly I'd adapted to the gruesome nature of this sim. I should be vomiting, too, but I was simply going through the motions. Doing what needed to be done to get the hell out of this place.

Finished, I slapped the Mark onto the slab like a bloody pancake, eager to see what it was.

Mark of Greater Health
+50% Maximum Health

Claim Mark for 300 Blood Points – Yes/No?

I barked a laugh. So that's why the guy lasted so long against me. No matter what damage he took, he kept on going. All because he had the health points to survive longer.

Well, now this was mine.

Grinning, I selected yes, and the Mark dissolved, reappearing across my mid-riff.

I explained what it was to Pullman.

"Wonderful, Captain," he said, looking grim. "Glad to see you've really thrown yourself into this sim. I know I don't have the stomach for it."

Someone has to, I thought, but didn't say it allowed. We weren't going to get out of this situation if I had to rely on Pullman, that was certain.

During the fighting, I missed a message.

Quest Completed: Slaughter the Enemy

10/10 Burned Men Slain

Reward: 2 skill points.

So I could get skill points, too. How many kinds of points were in this sim?

I glanced over my skills. My Butchery had increased to 6%, yet, I'd never even looked at it before.

Butchery: 6%

This skill allows you to do more damage when fighting three or more combatants at a time. +1 Weapon Damage will be applied for each 5% increment.

Well, that was an appropriate skill to have, all considered. My axe skill also increased to 5%, giving me a +1 damage bonus when using axes.

My Light Armor had increased to 2%, though I wasn't sure how, but I wasn't going to complain. Perhaps simply by wearing light armor in a fight caused it to go up.

When I tried to consider what to do, my eyes kept going to Butchery. There was no telling what weapon I would have at a given time, but Butchery would always give me a damage bonus, regardless.

With a mental shrug, I placed both into it, raising it to 8%.

As I'd been going over my skills, Pullman watched the screen which floated in front of me. "It really is a game, isn't it?" he said, amazed.

"Yes, a very disturbing one, too."

"Who made it?"

"Absolutely no clue, but I aim to find out," I said, dismissing the screen.

Pullman pointed at my hide shirt. "That thing your wearing is ripped to shreds."

I looked down. The hide had been cut to pieces, both the back and the front, barely hanging together by the cords.

Durability: Useless

Armor: 0 (Damaged beyond repair)

I cursed. So much for this thing. But it had served its purpose.

Removing it, I contemplated throwing it on the ground, then on a hunch, placed it on the slab. Nothing happened. I'd hoped there was a repair option of some sort.

Shrugging, I stored it, then took out another axe. I held it out to Pullman who recoiled. The slaves grouped near us gasped.

"What? You need to help with the fighting, so you need a weapon."

Pullman shook his head. "I can't. This harness won't let me."

I felt my annoyance return. "Just take the damn thing!" I said, and shoved it in his hand.

Suddenly, the harness he wore contracted, the various cords getting shorter. He dropped the axe and his pick and fell to the ground, doubled over. The cords yanked his wrists down to his sides at the waist, and folded his legs up, curling him into a fetal position.

He gasped with pain. "Captain!"

Surprised, I grabbed at one of the cords and tried to cut it. The cords cinched tighter and Pullman screamed, his face going red. "Stop! Don't!"

I jumped back, confused. One of the slaves, a woman, shook her head vigorously and waved her hands back and forth. *No.*

It took several seconds before the cords loosened. Pullman gasped for air. When he could finally breathe again, he said, "These things prevent us from using any weapons. Those bastards demonstrated it on me before. Pretty damned effective. If you try to cut them off, or remove them, they'll crush me."

So that's how they kept the slaves in line, I thought. Brutal, but effective. So much for my idea of having Pullman fight at my side.

It took a minute before he could stand, and I pulled him up. "Don't worry, Pullman. We'll get you out of that thing soon enough."

"When is that going to be?" he said, wiping spittle from his lips and gasping.

"I'm hoping once this phase that Chak is working on is finished there will be an option to exit."

"How do you know?"

"I don't. But we can't be stuck in this thing forever. Maybe once we complete whatever section we're in, we might be given a break." Honestly, I was just spit-balling. I had no clue whether that's what would happen. But I wanted to give Pullman some hope. We both needed it.

"Okay, so what next? We go to this Chak asshole?" Pullman said.

I nodded. "Follow me and stay close."

We moved out, the slaves right behind us. When we got close to where the large yellow mound could be seen in the distance, I made everyone stop.

To Pullman, I said, "I want you to hold back, I'll bring the others to Chak."

"Okay, but why?"

"You and I need to go check something out first."

"Captain, I don't mind playing slave and digging for this fool if it might help us get closer to getting out of this place."

"It's not that. There's something I need to make sure of first."

He shrugged, and I motioned for the five others to follow me, their picks in hand.

When I passed through the perimeter, Chak spotted me from the pedestal and waved me over.

As I got closer, I could see that a third of the dull red gems were now glowing brightly. Whatever he was up to, he was making progress.

Chak removed his hand from the pedestal and looked the group of slaves over. "Bah! Is this all you could manage? I need a dozen, at least!"

I felt my temper flare, but I kept it in check. "Hey, I went through a lot just to get these ones. I'll find more."

"You better!" he shouted. "The Molten God conspires against me! Look! He is flooding the chasm with his vile crap!"

In the distance I could easily make out sheets of lava cascading down the chasm walls. Barely any portion was untouched. Also, the lava was pooling up and slowly filling the chasm, forming a low red wall which was creeping toward us from all directions.

"This isn't good," I said. "We need to get out of here."

Suddenly, Chak stepped forward and slapped me across the face, catching me off guard. "Don't speak such cowardice! We are here to aid the Blood God, and we will go nowhere until we have done his bidding!" He raised his staff, and for a moment I was certain he was going to use it on me.

Not for the first time, I wanted to hit him. But I restrained myself. I knew that it wouldn't end well for me if I did. Besides, as much as I hated to admit it, I needed this fat pig.

"Sorry," I said. "Won't happen again."

The anger on his piggish features rippled away, and he lowered the staff. "Good. Now, you still have more slaves to get. Another seven.

We'll never make progress without them." He looked me over, noticed I was hurt, then placed his hand on my shoulder.

I hated having him so close to me, but had no other way to regenerate my health points quickly.

Chak leered over my body, and grunted when he saw the new Mark. "Ah, that's a good one to have. More health means you can kill more enemies. Need to keep my weapon in top form, eh, bitch?"

I didn't take the bait, and ground my teeth together.

Finished, he stood back. "Now stop wasting time, and go get me more slaves!" He turned and shouted at the group beside us. The slaves moved quickly and he corralled them over to the mound.

As I walked back to where Pullman was hiding, I watched as Chak instructed them to pick at the mound on the side with the pedestal. Eager to please, or perhaps simply terrified of being punished, the slaves jumped to the task, hacking away at the mound. Yellowish resin cracked and chipped under their pick axes.

It was obvious something was inside the mound. But what?

When I reached Pullman, he said, "What a piece of garbage that fat bastard is. I thought you were going to cut him up, right then and there."

"Not worth it," I said. "Besides, I think we need him. For now."

Pullman nodded. "I know there is another group of burned men with slaves. They were with us when I arrived, then went to go work somewhere else."

"Where?"

"No clue, but they headed further down the chasm from the spot you found me."

"How many?"

"Maybe six or seven slaves, and three of those burned bastards."

Only three burned men, I thought and smiled. That should be easy enough.

Pullman said, "One of them was a big brute, had one of those tattoo things across his shoulder. I think he's their leader. The others were scared of him."

"Okay, good. Come on, let's go."

"You haven't told me where we're going."

"You'll see."

We moved through the rocks, mindful not to be seen by Chak. I took us back down the path the Priest and I had originally arrived from. Soon enough, we got to the little clearing with the Life Crystal.

"So that's what it looks like, huh?" Pullman said, looking the glowing monolith over. "Kinda pretty. And this pool of blood is where you reappear at? Gruesome."

I motioned to the Life Crystal. "Put your hand on it and see if it asks you to bind to it."

The engineer arched a brow at me, but did as I asked. After a few seconds, he said, "Nothing. It doesn't come up with anything."

"Try again," I said, growing concerned.

He did, but still the same result. "What do you think it means? I can't respawn or whatever? Is that what your thinking?" He looked more worried than I felt.

"I don't know, but I suspect as much. I think the sim sees me as a character who the story is based around. Whereas you are..."

"Like a thing that dies and gives points," Pullman said. "Like those burned men back there. They won't be coming back, right?"

I nodded. If Pullman died, what then? Would he really die, or would he simply be logged out of the sim?

Frustrated, I said, "Well, I got my answer."

Pullman, despite his earlier display, was making an effort to be strong. "Hey, better the answer you don't like than no answer at all. That's what my commanding officer use to always tell us grunts."

We hurried back, talking along the way, trying to figure things out.

Pullman suddenly said, "I want to apologize for my behavior before."

"You don't need to," I said.

"No, I do. Since I arrived here, I haven't been myself. Everything scares me, and I have this overwhelming need to placate everyone. Like a damn dog."

"I've experienced something similar. I think the sim is effecting our minds somehow." I didn't want to admit it, but I had caught myself enjoying killing.

"What should we do? How can we fight it?"

"No idea, but we play along until this is done."

We moved on in silence, both lost in our thoughts.

When he entered the area of the mound, I brought Pullman over to Chak who was back at the pedestal. He didn't say a word, simply pointed at the area where the slaves were working. It appeared they were slowly gouging a section out of the mound, from the top all the way down to its base.

With a nod at me, Pullman joined the others. He knew the role he needed to play.

Before I left, I looked over the scene for a few moments; the slaves hacking away at the strange substance, Chak in a trance at the pedestal and the approaching line of lava in the distance.

Whatever was going to happen here, I knew it wasn't going to be good.

CHAPTER TWELVE

I jogged away from the area of the mound with no real idea where I was going. All I had were the vague directions Pullman had given me. Finding another six slaves appeared to be crucial to completing the phase Chak was working on, and might get me one step closer to getting out of this sim.

My eyes went to the clouds above. How long until Otto would be overhead? I had no idea, but it couldn't happen soon enough. Now that he'd given me hope, I desperately wanted more answers. Barring that, I'd take addition bits of information which would help better understand this screwed up world I was trapped on.

Part of me still bore a heavy worry, one that couldn't be ignored. If the Corena had been destroyed, we would be trapped here. If that were the case then the future would be as bleak as the clouds overhead.

Lost in my thoughts, I suddenly saw movement between the rock piles a short distance away and stopped. For a moment, it looked like a large boulder had trundled past. Carefully, I approached, keeping hidden as best I could. When I got close enough, I peaked around a tall column of stone.

It looked like a giant armadillo, low to the ground and with a large curved shell on its back. It stood on four stout legs, and its thick grey hide was covered in patches of fine brownish hair. Its head resembled a pig's, but with two large curved tusks protruding from its mouth which it was using to scrape at a section of ground.

What an ugly creature, I thought.

Juvenile Ghourda
Health: 100%
Magic: nil
Armor: 6

So this was the creature who's hide I'd been wearing. For a few moments I considered my options. Sure, I had to find those slaves quickly while there was still time, but I had a quest to skin this thing, and I really wanted another set of armor to wear.

Making up my mind, I darted through the rocks, trying to get closer. The thing didn't noticed as it was entirely focused on scraping at the ground, probably foraging.

A spear would've been nice at that moment; hit it from a distance then close in for the kill like the ancient hunters did.

Getting around behind it, I moved out from the rocks and slowly padded in its direction. The thing still hadn't noticed me, so busy with its duties. As I got close enough to swing, I hesitated. Where should I hit it? Having worn its hide, I knew it was tough enough to absorb an axe hit.

At that exact moment, the thing suddenly spun around and grunted in surprise.

Equally caught off guard, I tried to swing at its head and missed when it cantered back. Then it charged.

My swing took me a little off balance and I barely dodged out of the thing's way as it brushed past me. It turned around and charged again.

I was a little confused as to what to do. Up until now, I'd fought opponents who swung at me with weapons. This thing was short, squat and had no qualms about trying to run me over. I had not tactics to deal with it.

As it got close, I tried to swing sideways at it, figuring an overhead strike wouldn't slow its momentum. I hit it across the top of its head, slicing through the flap of an ear. But it still managed to get me.

Charging into me, it tossed its head sideways, knocking me to the side. I felt a tusk slice my lower abdomen, but it didn't pierce deeply.

It stopped a short distance away, and we eyed one another, each breathing heavily.

I hefted the axe in my hand, eager to kill the creature. "Come to momma," I said to it. "I need a new hide shirt."

As if encouraged by my words, it snorted loudly and charged.

When it was within range, I scooted to the side as fast as I could, and swung at its head. I managed to hit it hard just above the eyes, burying the blade deep.

This time, it ran a little further away before turning back at me. Blood gushed from the wound, covering its face and eyes. It shook its head, trying to see.

Sensing an opportunity, it was my turn to charge.

The ghourda seemed taken aback by this, and hopped on its forelegs in agitation. Then it, too, charged.

In less than a second we met at the middle. Unfortunately for me, my foot caught on a protrusion of rock and I stumbled.

With piggish glee, the creature snorted, and barreled right into me.

Thankfully, my fall and forward momentum allowed me to twist my body away. Just as one of its tusks was about to gore me in the stomach, the Mark of Dodge tingled. Defying all laws of gravity, I found myself tumbling over its head, tusks inches away, and bounced off its backside.

I fell to the ground hard, and scrambled to my feet. That was close. My guts would have been spilling all over the ground right then had it not been for the Mark.

The ghourda was angry now, but instead of charging, it ran up to slice at me with its tusks. I danced back each time, narrowly missing getting hit. I saw an opportunity and swung the axe at its head, using Bash.

The impact cracked it right on top of its head, piercing the skull. It wobbled on its legs, squealing loudly and thrashed about in pain.

I knew it was over. Two more swift strikes to the head and the creature collapsed to the ground, dead.

I stood panting for several minutes, trying to catch my breath. The thing was tough and had only been a juvenile. I hated to see what the adult version would be like in a fight.

Hunkering down next to the ghourda's body, I looked it over. I'd removed Marks before, but this seemed to be a different kind of operation entirely. Carefully, I worked the blade of the axe into its side and started to cut.

You have learned a new skill: Skinning

Allows for the proper removal of hides and various skins.

What? No incremental bonuses?

Suddenly, an outline appeared on the side of the creature's body, showing me where I should cut. It took longer than I wanted, but eventually I managed to remove two square flaps of hide, one from each side. The sinew was in its legs and took a while to properly remove, even with the glowing outline as a guide.

Finally finished, I admired my handy work.

You have completed a quest: Ghourda Skinning

2/2 units of Ghourda hide

1/1 unit of Sinew

Congratulations! You have learned a new schematic: Simple Ghourda Hide Shirt.

Good, I thought. I was going to need it as I felt completely naked without one.

I took the items over to a nearby glob of obsidian and placed them on its flat surface.

Simple Ghourda Hide Shirt

Requirements:

Units of Ghourda Hide: 2/2

Units of Sinew: 1/1

Craft this item for 200 Blood Points – Yes/No?

I said yes, and grinned as the shirt appeared. Satisfied with my newest creation I slipped it on. My armor was now at six; two for the hide shirt and four for the skull cap.

Now better protected, I moved on.

It took only a few minutes before I heard shouting ahead. It sounded like men in a heated argument. Finding cover, I picked my way forward until I was looking over a large flat plain. Far in the distance the approaching lava formed a solid red line, the air all around it wavering from the intense heat.

Close to me, about two dozen paces ahead, was a cage. It was round in shape, its bars made of stone, as if the entire structure had been carved from a single rock. Within cowered several people, both men and women. Slaves.

Standing next to the cage were two burned men. They were shouting at each other, and waving their weapons. One had an axe, the other wielded a weapon I'd not seen before; a sword which appeared to be made of bone. The one with the sword also had a Mark across his right shoulder.

A body lay next to them on the ground, blood seeping from fresh wounds. Another burned man, dead.

"The Molten God shall claim them!" the sword wielding man yelled. "Same as he shall claim this entire chasm!"

"You idiot!" the axe man yelled back. "They're good for trade! There are plenty of other slaves in the world for the Molten God to have, why waste these?"

Oh, what do we have here? I thought. From what Pullman had told me, I expected three burned men to fight. But with one dead and the other two at odds, I decided to wait a minute.

Sword Man pointed his weapon at the body on the ground. "He wouldn't listen, either. Do you want to end up like him?"

Axe Man shook his head, but didn't back down. "We shouldn't be fighting each other. The Blood God is the enemy. Him and his blighted followers."

"Then go fight 'em!" Sword Man said. "I'll stay here and ensure the Molten God gets his offerings!"

I surmised that the one with the sword wanted the slaves to be given to the advancing lava. A horrific way to die. But that wouldn't happen on my watch. I needed them more than the Molten God.

"No!" shouted Axe Man. "They're too valuable. Let's take them out of this place and trade them. No sense in having them die here."

Frustrated, the Sword Man suddenly punched him. "What kind of follower are you? They're for the Molten God, and that's final!"

Momentarily stunned by the punch, Axe Man roared and swung his weapon, slicing the Sword Man across his free arm. Sword Man shouted in pain, then swung his sword. Soon, they were in a full on fight.

Well this makes my job a lot easier, I thought, as I watched them hack at each other.

They swung and kicked at each other for several moments. Axe Man was getting the upper hand, landing most of his swings. But Sword Man was no slouch, either, having bloodied his opponent almost as badly.

Then, just when it looked like Axe Man might finish him off, Sword Man suddenly lunged forward and swung his sword crosswise. The weapon cut right through Axe Man's neck and sent his severed head spiraling away, where it fell to the ground and rolled.

Wow, I thought. That'd come out of nowhere.

Sword Man looked down at his fallen comrades. His own body was covered in cuts and gashes. Focusing on him brought up a little information screen showing his health was at 35%.

Perfect. Easy prey.

I waited just in case other Burned Men were nearby who may come to investigate the noise. The Sword Man fell to his knees, arms at his side. He looked despondent over what he'd done.

After a couple of minutes, I grew impatient. Besides, the wall of lava was creeping ever closer.

I moved out from behind the rocks, keeping the cage between me and the Sword Man. As I got closer to it, the slaves within saw me, but didn't make a sound. They watched me wide-eyed. Was I their rescuer, or just another master for them to be bound to? I was both, actually.

Creeping around the cage, I positioned myself so the burned man's back was to me. When I was certain he hadn't detected me, I sprinted forward, axe held high. My aim was to crack him over the back of the head.

The distance between us shrank, and my heart beat hard in my chest with anticipation. This was going to be easy.

Then, right when I was about to bring the axe down, the burned man sprang to his feet and turned. This messed up my swing, but I did bury my axe deep into his left shoulder, cutting through bone.

The man shrieked, but despite the pain, suddenly brought his sword up with blinding speed.

I didn't even feel the blade pass through my neck. In the next instant, the world swirled as my severed head spun through the air.

It hit the ground and bounced, and I felt nothing. As my head settled against a rock, I could see my headless body fall over, gushing blood from the neck.

The burned man collapsed to his knees, clutching at the handle of the axe in his shoulder, screaming.

Then my vision brightened, and a whiteness consumed me.

You have been slain.

CHAPTER THIRTEEN

The whiteness shifted and changed. Then the familiar yellow and purple colors formed, and I felt blood slosh against my face.

I tore through the membrane of the blood pool, and flopped onto the ground, coughing and hacking.

Well, damn, I thought. He cut my head off!

Disoriented, I sat up, trying to wipe blood from my eyes.

I'd been so convinced he'd be an easy kill. To have that snatched away from me in such a horrific manner took a few moments to process. Impulsively, I checked my neck. The memory of the sword cutting through my throat made me shiver all over.

A sudden realization that I was burning up made me take stock of my surroundings.

Lava was spilling over the rock walls at the other end of the clearing, submerging the Life Crystal. The slow moving wave bubbled toward me, and I scrambled to get away from it.

I watched in shock as the pool was covered as well, the blood within evaporating in an instant.

Looking about, I could see lava was advancing over the surrounding area, and for a moment I feared I might be cut off from escape.

Quickly, I ran out into the pathway to find lava slowly heaving over the walls on one side. Panicking, I sprinted down the path as the lava reached the ground.

Ahead, the lava had nearly covered the left turn I needed to pass through. Seeing no other choice, I leapt over the flowing mass of the stuff to land on the other side, and fell to the ground. My head came within a foot of a protrusion of lava, the heat searing the side of my face.

Shouting in pain, I got to my feet and ran into the first clearing where I'd killed the two burned men.

Lava was spilling into it as well, but thankfully hadn't reached the other side.

I ran as fast as my bare feet could carry me.

The Life Crystal was gone. The blood pool – my respawn point – was gone. What did that mean if I died again? Would I pop up back there, under all the lava?

As I navigated through the rocks, I glanced over my body. My blood covered skin had no Marks on it. I'd lost them both. Add to that the loss of a whole bunch of Blood Points, and I was beyond angry when finally reaching the area with the giant mound.

The slaves were toiling away, almost feverishly. It appeared the deep trench in the yellow excretion was getting deeper, and wider.

I ran over to the inventory stone and took out an axe and a pair of green mushrooms. As I did, I saw Pullman working diligently away at the huge trough, playing his part. He looked over at me with concern and I shook my head.

Chak was standing with his hand on the pedestal, eyes half-closed. It appeared most of the red gems were now alight.

Back on the path to the Sword Man and the caged slaves, I cursed myself over and over. Replaying the scenario of my gruesome death in my mind didn't present any other solution to how I could have avoided it. Either that guy got extremely lucky with his swing, or something else was going on.

Roughly halfway there, I gulped down both mushrooms, trying to keep my Power as high as possible. Fortunately, I didn't run into anyone or anything else to hinder my way.

I arrived back at the wide open area, and snuck up to a pile of rocks to look.

The lava was a lot closer now, having made progress at an alarming speed. It'd already spread into the clearing, and was advancing quickly. The slaves were still in the cage, watching the approaching lava, and whimpering.

To my relief, the bodies of the burned men were still there. The skaggs hadn't claimed them, yet. Perhaps the lava kept them away. Also, my axe, hide shirt, and skull cap were gone, maybe as part of the price of my resurrection.

I moved out from my hiding spot and down to where the Sword Man's body was sprawled on the ground. Sightless eyes stared up at me. At least he paid a price for killing me. I grabbed his sword.

You have taken an item: Fine Bone Sword (Enhanced)
Durability: Good
Damage: 8-12
+5 Enhanced Damage
Tradable

Oh, hey, this was interesting. Talk about damage. What was the enhanced stuff about? I'd ask Chak later.

I noticed something was dangling at his hip. It was a large brown key. Pulling it loose, I could see it was made of stone. I went to the cage, where the slaves gaped at me in fear.

"Don't worry," I said, finding the lock in the cage's door and inserting the key. "I'll get you out of here."

The lock clicked, and the door swung open. Timidly, the slaves filed out, then stood in a group, watching me for instructions.

Ignoring them, I went over to Sword Man's body and stared down at the Mark on his uninjured shoulder. That was my Mark. I'd earned it.

Glancing at the advancing lava told me I wouldn't have time to work here. To free a hand, I dropped the axe and hefted the big guy onto my shoulder.

"Follow me and stay close," I told the slaves. Together we hurried away from the clearing.

About five minutes later, I spotted a crafting table, its obsidian contrasted against a outcropping of white rocks. Commanding the slaves to wait, I dumped the body next to it, then set about removing the Mark. I was very curious to know what it was.

Finished, I dumped the slab of skin onto the obsidian.

Mark of Decapitation

+50% chance an attack with a bladed weapon will decapitate an opponent.

Claim this Mark for 300 Blood Points – Yes/No?

So that's how he did it! Well, it was mine now.

But it would have to wait as I'd lost all my Blood Points.

Grumbling, I put it in an inventory stone. How long would it be before I could start loping people's heads off?

Shaking my head with frustration, I led the slaves away. Behind us, the lava advanced and was getting faster.

Finally returning to the mound, I found chaos.

The slaves were standing at the top of the mound in a cluster, Pullman amongst them. At the base, by the pedestal, Chak was sparring with two burned men. The blood priest was keeping them at bay with the staff.

Blinking in surprise, I sprinted in his direction.

One of the men must have seen me, and turned to look. Chak lunged forward with the staff, thumping it against the man's chest. The burned man shrieked, as the acid rushed across his body.

The other man had seen enough and turned to flee, but not before I brought my new sword down upon his head, using Bash. His skull cleaved in two and fell to the ground next to his companion, who was shrieking as his body dissolved.

You have learned a new skill: Swords

I looked to Chak, half-expecting a thanks.

"Where have you been?" he roared. "It's almost time! Protect the perimeter!"

Before I could respond, he ran off to scream at the new slaves, ordering them to work.

I could easily see the advancing lava flows from all directions. It would only be a matter of time before they arrived at this spot.

The slaves had made tremendous progress. The slice was now deep into the mound. Through its opaque yellowish resin, I could see something large at its center. Whether it was the play of the light of the advancing lava or my imagination, but I thought I saw movement.

"Bitch!" Chak bellowed. He pointed at a burned man who'd appeared. "Kill!"

I ran over to take care of the intruder, something I was getting quite good at.

The fight was brief, my motions almost on a kind of murderous autopilot. With the burned man dead at my feet, I realized something.

Quickly, I ran to the inventory stone and removed the Mark of Decapitation. Slapping it on the table, I paid 300 Blood Points to claim it.

I felt the satisfying itch of the Mark drawn across my right shoulder and down over my breast. Finally.

Suddenly, a shout from the mound made me whip around. The slaves were scampering away from the gouge. From my vantage point, I could easily see something inside moving and thrashing. Whatever it was, it was trying to escape.

Chak was wide-eyed with glee. His hand on the pedestal, he watched as the thing within the mound fought to get free. "Yes!" he cried. "It is time!" The last dull gem winked on. All gems glowed brightly on the pedestal.

From within the mound, something screeched.

I felt a shiver race up my spine. What in the hell was it?

The sudden appearance of another burned man forced me to look away. Only after I'd practically butchered him did I turn back.

Something was breaking free of the mound, pushing its way through the gouge the slaves had created for it. I saw something white poke out, its obscured body rippling and pulsating. It was long and fat, but I still couldn't make out what it was.

Chak suddenly screamed, dropped his staff and fell to his knees.

I ran over, confused. Looking around, I didn't see any burned men. Had he been attacked?

He clutched at his arm, its hand covered in bright red beetles which where burying themselves into his flesh. The pedestal was bare. It hadn't been gems that were lighting up, but these insects.

Without thinking, I stepped forward to help, but Chak practically spat at me.

"Don't you dare!" he shrieked, his eyes on the glowing red beetles. The things seemed to have settled into place, their bodies resembling grotesque holiday lights. "This is needed to control it!" he looked away from the ruin of his hand to the mound.

From within the gap, the giant white creature burst forth. The yellow resin of the mound cracked and shattered as it finally forced its way through. Freed, it slunk forward, the segmented rings of its body rippling with the effort.

A gaped in horror. A maggot. A giant maggot bigger than a shuttlecraft.

What was going on? I thought, fighting back the creeping terror I felt.

Pullman ran up to me, his eyes wide. "What the hell is that?"

"No clue," I said, watching the monster squirm forward.

A large black orifice at its front end opened and closed like a beak. Suddenly, it twisted around and snapped up a screaming slave.

We watched, stunned, as the poor man was eaten alive, gobbled up by the beak. To our continued horror, the opaque body of the monster showed the pulped slave travel down its length to its center.

Beside me, Pullman retched.

My eyes were drawn to Chak, who stood holding his hand with the beetles in front of him. "Come, my beauty!" he shouted at the thing. "I shall show you the way!"

As if it could understand him, the maggot squirmed forward.

All three of us had to backpedal quickly as the monster's body slammed down on the pedestal in its path, crushing it. It kept coming forward, seemingly draw by Chak's hand.

"What should we do?" Pullman said, as we backed away from the thing.

A burned man suddenly appeared on the opposite side, directly in the path of the creature. The maggot suddenly moved with terrifying speed, twisting its head around to grab him. In seconds, the burned man was eaten, the shadowy outline of his body traveling down the length of the thing to join the others.

"I'd say we should stay out of its way," I said.

The thing moved forward, trailing after Chak.

The Blood Priest screamed at me. "Clear the way for us, Berserker! We need to leave this place, and quick!" He spoke through clenched teeth, the pain of his hand must've been unbearable.

I saw another burned man appear. Whether they were coming to attack or being driven to this spot by the lava, I didn't care. All I knew is that they would each die by my hand.

"Keep the slaves away from its mouth, and stay close to me if you can."

Pullman nodded, bewildered. He ran off, calling to the slaves.

I ran at the latest burned man, who suddenly stopped to stare in amazement at the huge maggot. Without making any effort to defend himself, I swung my sword and aimed for his neck.

The Mark tingled on my shoulder as I sliced his head off.

But I didn't have time to admire my handy work as another burned man appeared and I ran over to take care of him.

All the while, Chak led the huge maggot along, away from the mound and up the length of the chasm. The ground was rising ever so slightly in that direction, leading to the opposite end which formed a natural stony bridge partway up the wall. Was that where the priest intended the thing to go?

Around us the lava got closer. It was perhaps less than a twenty meters at its closest.

Our little procession worked its way up the chasm, slowly climbing the incline of the bridge. I lost count the number of burned men I killed. Sometimes, I'd luck out and lop off a head; most times, I'd quickly dispatch them with a series of calculated swings. They never came at me in groups. Always solo, which led me to believe they were simply trying to escape the lava, not launch a coordinated attack.

Yet, I was taking a lot of damage, and my health was dropping fast. It wouldn't be long before I couldn't fight.

The maggot squirmed forward, every once in a while scooping up the body of one of the men I killed and devouring it. Each time, the pulped body slide down to join the others at its middle. It was like watching a morbid version of a play with shadow-puppets.

So caught up in fighting, we arrived at the end of the chasm before I realized it. The land bridge angled up the side of the chasm wall where it ended halfway. There wasn't a tunnel or any means of escape.

But Chak still led the thing, until the monstrous creature could climb no further up the incline, and had stopped. After a few seconds, its body began to quiver and shake.

Around us, the chasm was now a sea of lava, the path we'd traveled completely covered. Only the occasional outcropping of rock could be seen poking out of the molten lake.

I was at death's door. Fortunately, there were no more burned men to fight because there was no place else for them to appear from. Just lava as far as you could see. I needed healing, and quick.

I staggered toward Chak, my body screaming with pain all over. My health had dropped to 12%, and I was bleeding from my wounds. I didn't have long left.

The priest didn't notice my approach, so enthralled with the gyrating maggot. Within its opaque flesh, I could see the various parts of the corpses had now congealed into on giant lumpy form at its center. The form appeared to be moving, pulsating.

The slaves cowered at the edge of the bridge with nowhere else to go. Pullman stared at me, wide-eyed, waiting for my signal to help, but I shook my head. There was nothing he could do.

"It's time!" Chak said, his eyes wide and feverish. "The culmination of all my work! My doing! Oh, how the Blood God will reward me!"

I could barely hear him through the ringing in my ears. "I need healing." Apparently, the obvious needed to be stated.

Chak blinked and turned to look me over. "You dare to interrupt at a time like this? Stupid bitch!"

Before I knew it, he slapped me hard across the face. I rocked back, but kept my footing. Pullman took a few steps toward me, but I waved at him to stop. He reluctantly obeyed.

The Blood Priest raged at me. "Do you not see what is happening? It is time for his return! He shall walk the Realm again and all shall tremble at his power. And I was the one who made it happen. Chak! The world shall fear my name!"

I had enough of this twit, and said, "We did it."

This brought him up short, "What? We did it? No, *we* did not. I did it. Me. You were but a tool to be used to aid on the journey. A tool I crafted to be used. And like all tools, they are thrown away when no longer of use." He glared at me, challenging me to speak.

Of course I willing took the bait. "I'm not a tool, I'm a weapon. The Blood God's weapon. You said so yourself."

"Bah! I only told you what you needed to hear. How else could I make such an insolent wench do my bidding? And you did it all! Ha! I expected nothing less from such a stupid bitch."

My anger flared. When I spoke, I made a point of keeping my voice even. "Don't call me that, again."

The fat man laughed, his sweaty belly jiggling. "I knew it! Such weakness! Such insolence! Well, no matter. The Blood God knows it was me. I guided us to this point. I was the one who masterminded it all. It is I who will become his Herald. Not you."

Behind him, the maggot's body shivered and quaked. A reddish bio-luminescence glowed from within, darkening its interior. Its outer flesh boiled and rippled, like it was being cooked alive. The large dark form inside moved.

But Chak didn't notice, so wrapped up in castigating me. "And as his Herald, it will be my task to create more tools, like you. But ones who are more obedient. I shall create hundreds! We will march across the Realm and do the Blood God's bidding!"

I said nothing during this tirade, only staring at him, waiting.

He seemed to realize he was screaming, and toned it down. His piggish eyes looked me over. "Look at you. A broken tool. No matter, you have served your purpose." He hefted his staff and grinned when I flinched.

"Think of the hell you shall endure," he said. "I will kill you and you shall respawn back at the life crystal which is deep within that lake of lava. An instant after your rebirth, you will be burned alive in seconds! Then you will respawn again, and again you will die in delicious agony. Over and over the process will continue. For how long? Millennia perhaps? Only the gods know."

I didn't react, not wanting him to give him any satisfaction.

Seeing my inaction, he leaned forward so close, when he spoke, I felt his hot, putrid breath on my face. "Good bye, you stupid bi-."

I decapitated him.

It was simple enough; a solid backhand swing from left to right. I felt the satisfying snick of the blade easily cutting through his spinal cord just above his slumped shoulders.

His fat head spun away and bounced along the ground where it then rolled over the edge of the bridge. It landed in the boiling lava below, facing up, his lips still contorted with his final word. Then it sank beneath and was gone.

Chak's body gushed blood from the stump of its neck and collapsed heavily to the ground. The staff fell from its hand, clattered along the stone ground, then slid into a crevasse.

I looked down at my handy work. "Told you not to call me that," I said.

Pullman ran up beside me. "Captain! Are... are you okay?"

"Just great, Pullman," I said, then carefully knelt next to the body, hissing at my various pains. It took only a couple of minutes to slice the Mark from Chak's body, a task I'd become quite experienced with.

Pullman watched in horrified silence. Part of me wished he was stronger. But I knew he didn't have the stomach for this place, and never would.

With the Mark in hand, I eased up to my feet, waving Pullman's offer of help. "I can do this on my own," I said. There was a slab of obsidian perched at the edge of the bridge and I hobbled over to it, Pullman in my wake.

"What's going to happen now?" he said, looking back at the headless body. "Didn't we need him to finish this?"

"No, we didn't need him," I said, and dropped the Mark onto the table with a bloody splat. "I'll finish this."

A message appeared.

Mark of Healing

This Mark grants the wearer the ability to recover health points on themselves or others via touch.

Maximum 5 health points every 5 seconds.

Cost: 10 Blood Points per health point.
Claim Mark for 500 Blood Points – Yes/No?

"Damn right, yes," I said.

The slab of skin sizzled away, then reappeared across my left shoulder and down my chest. I then spent another 480 Blood Points to fully heal. The sensation was wonderful, almost addicting.

Through all of this, Pullman remained silent. Part of me wondered if it was our differing strengths that placed us in our roles in this sim; me as a fighter, he as a slave. Could it be that simple?

The cluster of slaves suddenly gasped, and I turned to see what it was.

The maggot was expanding, its middle banded segments splitting like old tire treads. Blood spilled from the wounds; first a series of trickles, then a gushing flood. It was as if the massive thing was emptying out of everything inside.

Despite myself, I moved closer, mindful of the rivers of blood gushing along the ground. This was what Chak had been waiting for – died for. To him, it was something wonderful to behold. To me it was a grotesque nightmare.

Then, something reached out from the gaping wound. Hands. They gripped the thick flaps of maggot flesh and pulled them wider, making room. Suddenly, a man stepped out of the dead creature to stand on the ground.

I gazed in awe. He was huge; a giant easily three times my height. Blood flowed over his body, and as it cleared, I could see exposed tendons and muscles. He had not skin.

Lidless eyes rotated within sockets to gaze about, and, despite lacking lips, his mouth morphed into a skeletal smile.

"I live," he said, his voice deep and booming.

This was him. The big guy. The one all this crap I'd gone through was about.

The Blood God.

CHAPTER FOURTEEN

For a few moments I found myself at a loss for words. Real or not, what did one say to a god, anyways?

What was I suppose to do next? Was this the end? Could I go home now?

Turned out, I didn't have to say anything at all.

The goliath looked in my direction, and spoke one word.

"Herald."

I felt a sudden rush of euphoria, like a cool, gentle breeze washing over my soul. A peace fell upon me, then. I can't explain it, but I knew standing there, that it was exactly where I was meant to be.

Standing before my god.

I drunkenly smiled. He was looking at me. So beautiful, so powerful, so perfect. It was such an honor to be in his presence I wanted to cry. Tears fell down my blood-stained cheeks.

He was here. Finally.

The Blood God turned his magnificent gaze to the panicking slaves, who clung to each other in fear.

"Herald," he said, his voice making my knees quiver in ecstasy. "I am in need of blood."

Suddenly, my talent-tree appeared. A new tab was created next to the others, this one marked Herald. At the center was an icon for a new talent. It was the picture of a naked woman, armed with twin daggers, leaping into a group of enemies. She looked just like me.

Blood Harvest (No Talent Point Required)

Cost: 15 Power

Cooldown: 8 hours

Sends a Herald into a savage rage, attacking nearby enemies. All Blood Points earned from kills during it's use go directly to the Blood God.

Duration: 45 seconds

+80% success to hit targets

+50% all physical damage dealt

2 x Reflex Attribute

-40% Armor Rating

-40% to all defensive abilities and skills

-100% Blood Points gained

"What is-," I started to say, my mind in a strange haze.

The Blood God pointed at the slaves. "Harvest for me."

Use Blood Harvest

I ran screaming at the slaves.

In the span of a heart beat, I crossed the distance and fell upon them. None resisted me, even if they could. I hacked and bashed and kicked and bit and tore through them all. Before thirty seconds had even passed they were all dead, but I kept attacking, screeching and yelling like a blood-crazed maniac.

Finally, forty-five seconds passed, and the ability went into cool down.

The moment it did, I collapsed to my knees, covered in fresh blood and gore. I looked around at what I'd done. Butchery. Pure savage butchery.

I spotted Pullman's severed head next to me, bloody face upturned. His expression was one of surprise.

What did I just do? I had no control over myself. It was like someone else controlled my body.

"Good," the Blood God said.

I looked at him and I knew then that what I'd done was right. His will had been fulfilled and that was all that mattered.

He raised a hand to me. "Come. Because of your gift, we can leave this place."

I stood and quickly moved to his side. Being close to him gave me a warmth to my spirit I'd never experienced before, and didn't want to end.

Around us, the lava roiled and hissed, threatening to surge upward and overtake the bridge we stood on.

But the Blood God didn't care. He raised a hand toward the chasm wall before us. A glowing red beam burst from his upraised palm and struck the rocky wall. The light quickly crept over its surface and enveloped a wide section all the way to the top edge.

Then he closed his hand and the light winked out.

The chasm wall was gone. Beyond was a vast open desert, covered in orange haze.

We walked forward, up and over the bridge and through the huge gap.

Behind us, I could hear a rumbling and hissing. I worried something may attack my God, and I started to turn.

"Do not look back, Herald," the Blood God said. "The Molten God rages at a missed opportunity. Do not give him any satisfaction."

I did as he said, but ignoring the cataclysmic sounds was difficult.

We stopped a short distance away from the edge of the chasm. The orange haze was everywhere, and I could see a series of massive pyramids poking through in the distance.

The Blood God stopped and looked down at me. Even though he lacked expression, I could feel his love. "You have done well, Herald. But you must do more."

"I will," I murmured.

"With my rebirth, a new dawn breaks upon the Realm. A blood dawn."

His words were melodic to my ears, like a listening to a lover.

"My enemies will know of my arrival, and they conspire against me."

Hearing this made me angry, creating red hot rage that I could barely contain.

"They must be kept at bay, and weakened, while my strength returns. Go out unto the Realm and slay any that you find."

"I will," I said, my voice barely a whisper. He wanted me to do his will. He trusted no one else. Just me!

He said, "I will send you tasks as they are required. For now, I must go. I am exposed here."

With a wave of a hand, the ground suddenly swelled next to us. It cracked open and a red membrane ballooned outward forming a huge pustule of blood.

He walked to it and I felt my heart sink at the thought of him leaving.

Stopping, he turned and looked at me. "Remember Herald, we are one." And with that he walked into the pustule which moved to envelop him. With a rumble, the giant membrane shrank back into the ground and was gone.

My knees gave out and I crumpled to the ground, exhausted. It was like I'd been propped up by strings since the moment the Blood God emerged.

My head swam. What the hell just happened?

I recalled the massacre I'd just committed and the butchering of Pullman. I retched until my stomach couldn't produce anything more. He was gone. No respawn for him. So was he really dead? Or removed from the game and was now sitting in a comfy chair somewhere, drinking a cocktail and laughing at me?

"Captain, can you hear me?"

It was Otto!

"Yes! I can hear you!" I said, relieved to be speaking with him again. "Gimme a sitrep." Give me something else to think about other than being a crazed murderer.

"I have good news!"

"You found a way out of this nightmare?" I said, hopeful.

"Negative. Well, not yet. But I may have something which could make that happen. I found the Corena."

"What?" I was stunned. Hope against hope, I'd wondered if I'd ever learn its fate. "Where is it?" And, more importantly, was my real body still inside?

"It is on the other side of the planet. Almost exactly opposite of where you are now."

My hope faded a little. "Is it damaged?"

"I can't say for certain. That section of the world has not been rendered, but it appears to be one kilometer below the surface. I can detect its outline, and it appears to me intact."

"Any life signs?"

"Unclear, Captain. But we can assume that it is possible you and the others are sequestered inside."

"Maybe," I said. We really didn't know anything. Our bodies could be at the core of the planet, or somewhere else entirely. But this was something I could hold onto, work with. "Okay, so what do you think, I have to walk all the way there to investigate?"

"I'm afraid so, Captain. We have no other means of inspecting the site where the ship is, so we won't know until the area is rendered. And for that to happen, you need to be present."

"How far are we talking here?" The planet had expanded from its original two thousand kilometers in diameter. How worse could it get?

"A direct line would cover roughly 28,000 kilometers.

So far! I blanched, taking in the vast orange desert before me. The distance to the pyramids was maybe three or four kilometers. Past them, who knew what was out there yet to be created for my unending enjoyment. Tens of thousands of kilometers of fun to be had.

"Damn!" I said, and paced around in agitation. Such a journey was going to be further complicated by whatever tasks the Blood God gave me, not including other quests that would be thrown in my path.

"Captain, are you okay? I'm about to move out of range. The storm clouds are also becoming more troublesome with our communication."

"Yeah, I'm good. Just peachy." Right.

"Captain, there is one other thing I've found."

A teleporter to the other side of the planet? "And that is?"

"I've detected an unusual life sign a short distance from your current location."

"What kind of life sign?"

"Unknown. It's located within the pyramid structures to the east."

I looked in their direction again, half-expecting to see someone there waving at me. "Who? A crew member?"

"Unknown. But it may be worth investigating. Captain, I will try and contact you soon. I'm worried -."

A cavalcade of lightning shattered the sky above, and Otto's voice went quiet.

I stared at the pyramids, and the vast desert beyond them. Well, every journey must start with a single step.

I walked forward a short distance until I reached the spot where the chasm rocks ended and the desert began. The two biomes pressed against each other to form a distinct line. Further ahead, maybe thirty paces, was a tall glowing crystal, sticking out of the dry desert ground.

A Life Crystal.

As I stepped over the line and onto the desert sand, a message appeared.

You have left the tutorial zone.

Additional abilities have been made available for unlocking in your talent-trees.

Whoa. Really? All that crap I'd just suffered through was only a tutorial? It made me worry about what more challenging aspects of this sim I've yet to encounter. What was out there waiting for me?

I reached the glowing monolith and stared up at it. It was identical to the one back in the clearing, buried under lava.

I touched its surface.

Broken Desert Life Crystal

Bind yourself to this Crystal – Yes/No?

"Yes," I said, and sighed. How many times would I be respawning here?

You are now bound to the Broken Desert Life Crystal.

I looked off at the pyramids, they were a long ways away. But having little choice in the matter, I kept going. At some point I'd get there, I wasn't in any hurry.

Several steps from the Life Crystal another message appeared, and this one brought me chills.

It said:

Welcome to the Realm of Carnage

I hoped this world wouldn't live up to the name.

Turns out, I was very, very wrong.

Zyra's blood-soaked nightmare continues in

Bitch Berserker 2: Realm of Carnage

Kingdom Level One
(Kingdom Series Book 1)

A broken kingdom for a reluctant king.

Robert was content with his life as a night-shift janitor. No stress, no worries, and no responsibilities. But this idyllic existence is turned upside down when he suddenly finds himself trapped inside a fantasy Role Playing Game.

Confused and alone he must find a way to escape back to his own world and, more importantly, to his daughter. But to do that he must take up the biggest responsibility of all:

To rule a kingdom.

AVAILABLE NOW

Shadow Gambit
<u>(Shadow For Hire Series Book 1)</u>

An impossible quest for a legendary item.

I love questing for loot.

And the more difficult the quest, the greater the reward.

So when I'm offered a chance to retrieve the ultimate treasure of all, I signed up.

Yet no one warned me the task would be impossible. Against overwhelming odds I'm also expected to defeat an ancient evil - one with the power of a god.

But you know what?

Some loot is worth risking it all.

AVAILABLE NOW

<u>Blackout</u>
<u>A Terrifying Dystopian Thriller</u>

147

The nightmare begins

In one fell swoop, civilization is changed forever.

No one is unaffected, few are prepared.

Some become survivors, others - easy prey.

Only the strong, and crazy, will survive.

Through the blood and chaos, civilization will be permanently transformed.

And it all begins with one terrifying moment, when the lights go out and never come back on.

Blackout.

AVAILABLE NOW

Author Page

Check out my author page for
other titles in my catalog and new releases.
Adam Drake Author Page[1]

---

1. https://books2read.com/ap/RQ3qV8/Adam-Drake